Loan Some

A NOVELLA

MEGAN McLACHLAN

SEREALITIES PRESS

www.serealities.com

ISBN: 0692308091
ISBN 13: 9780692308097
Library of Congress Control Number: 2014918168
Serealities Press
Birmingham, AL

PART I:

"Things are not always what they seem."

Chapter 1

"People just aren't going to libraries anymore."

Mr. Lopper's words rang through Vera's ears as she packed up her belongings in a brown cardboard box on her last day of work at the Albright County Library. "This generation's idea of a card catalog is an ironic antique you see in some hipster's studio apartment."

Mr. Lopper was right. Library activity had dwindled in recent months, years even. The children Vera used to help discover *Anne of Green Gables* and *The Hardy Boys* were now exploring books for themselves on their parents' iPads and Kindles.

In fact, part of the reason why Mr. Lopper's words rang through her ears was because no one was in the building. No protestors, no good-byes. The closing of this library was just a fact of life, like a small, defenseless animal being pounced on in an issue of *National Geographic*.

"Welp," said Mr. Lopper, a man Vera had called her boss for more than ten years, "I'm just about packed up." He emerged from his office with a set of James Patterson novels he'd been eyeing since they'd received word the library was closing. "You ready?"

"Could I just have a minute?" Vera whispered, almost as if she were apologizing.

"Take all the time you need." Mr. Lopper left through the series of library doors, each one reverberating after every shut.

Vera's heels click-clocked as she walked through the library aisles, recalling what books used to be on the empty shelves. So much dust. As a child, she had loved the idea of a library—the way everything was organized in its place, easy to find and enjoy. She adored jumping into stories and putting herself in the roles of everyone from the protagonist to the villain. When she was a child, while others were playing house, pretending to be teachers or doctors, Vera wanted to become a character in a book.

She let out a sneeze before wiping a tear from her eye.

"I don't see what the big deal is," said Jeffrey in between bites of steak at dinner in Vera's apartment. "Shit like this happens. You have to move on."

Jeffrey was a chubby mook of a man, whose schlubbiness had started out endearing but had stayed on him like a grimy film. Even tonight he was dressed in sweatpants and a ratty T-shirt, while she was still in her last-day-of-work clothes, a pencil skirt and white boat-neck blouse. It couldn't look like a more awkward date.

Despite all of the effort she had put into the steaks, Vera pushed the plate away.

"Why aren't you eating?" he asked.

"I'm upset."

"You haven't been eating lately."

Actually, with the stress of losing her job, Vera had been eating what felt like a ton. It was only today that she suddenly lost her appetite.

"People stare at us when we walk down the street," he said.

"What? Do you think I look sick?"

"I always liked the way we balanced each other out. We were both a bit rounder. It made me feel good about myself. But you've been looking better lately, and I don't know if I can do this."

"Do what?"

"I can't be with someone thinner than me." He took a bite of steak, the piece dangling out of his mouth like a rock climber on the edge of a cliff.

She couldn't stop focusing on that half-masticated scrap, the way it continued to cling to his lip for no reason, other than collective will. She and Jeffrey had had a rough go of it over the past couple of months, yet she always returned to him out of comfortable habit. But today was different.

"Well, then," said Vera, "since you're taking up so much space, why don't you leave?"

It took a few moments for the temerity to register, even as Vera stared at him, eyebrows raised.

"Now?" He continued to work on that piece in his mouth. "Can't I finish?"

"I'll give you a to-go box."

With a squeak of the chair legs against her kitchen floor, she got up, grabbed a piece of Tupperware from her cabinet, and threw the rest of his dinner in the box, all while he was sitting there, still chewing. He realized her urgency when she stood at the doorway with the box in her hands, waiting for him to follow. He rose from his chair, conjuring the same squeaking sound of wood against linoleum, and leisurely strolled to the doorway, opening the door and pausing at the entrance. He grabbed the to-go container.

"I'll return the Tupperware later—"

She slammed the door in his face.

Weeks later, sunlight poured through Vera's bedroom window as she rolled toward her eyeglasses next to the clock on the nightstand.

It's three o'clock, she said to herself. *I suppose it's time to put on a bra.*

This had become her routine. Stay up late reading, sleep until the early afternoon, all usually without a bra. Vera had submitted her resume to every library within a hundred-mile radius, but no one was hiring. Thankfully, her depression sought solace in the likes of Henry James and Zora Neale Hurston instead of Jim Beam and White Zinfandel. Otherwise, she might have had a problem.

Before tumbling out of bed, she grabbed the phone on her nightstand and checked her messages to see if any job prospects had called back. *Nothing.* Only her father, who kept calling to find out how she was doing, had left her any. He knew she had lost her job, ended a relationship, and was going through some sort of shame spiral, although Vera liked to think of it as a shame curvature. She didn't want to call him back until she was feeling more like herself, and at the moment, all she wanted to do was curl up and hide from the world forever.

After going through her father's messages and feeling guilty for not responding just yet, Vera ventured to her desk, plopping herself down into a chair while waiting for her laptop to warm up. She hated her symbiotic reliance on this machine, the way it both killed her profession yet held future job opportunities. She checked her e-mail for job application responses but instead got lost in her personal messages.

She had one from a Betsey Burrows in Alberta, Canada. Vera's eyes lit up. She had sent this message months ago, during one of her occasional phases where she felt the need to find her mother. She was more excited about the prospects of this response than any of the job ones.

"Hello, Vera," it said. "Thank you for reaching out. However, I'm sorry to tell you that I did not give birth to a baby thirty-some years ago. Good luck in your search. I'm sorry I can't be of more help. Sincerely, Betsey Burrows."

From time to time, Vera would get into a mood where she felt the desire to search for her mother. Since she'd had a lot of time on her hands lately, she started doing more Google searches and research. She wanted to ask her father, but she rarely asked him about her mother. She knew it was a sore subject.

She moved on to the other messages in her inbox. One message was from Jeffrey at 2:00 a.m.: "Hey, you up?" was all it said.

She knew what *that* meant. Since the breakup, she had occasionally received these late-night messages from him, when he was lonely and vulnerable after reading his share of graphic novels over boxed wine. *Delete message.*

She saw another response, from a job she had applied to at Loan Some, a company that described itself as "a library of characters for every occasion." She wasn't quite sure what that meant, but it had "library" in the description, so naturally she had responded with a resume and cover letter.

"We'd love to sit down and talk with you," said the e-mail. "Can you come to Market Street Place around 4 today?"

Checking the alarm clock on her dresser—3:07!—Vera responded and put on some real clothes, ones that didn't have Chinese takeout stains on them, for the first time in days.

At Market Street Place, a bistro in town, Vera saw a man at a corner table who looked like he rarely ventured into the twenty-first century, much less a bar. He had a thick, uncle-like mustache, a stale shirt tucked into brown trousers, and reading glasses that hung on a chain around his neck.

Vera sat at a table adjacent to his, as she wasn't sure whether he was the person she was meeting.

"Vera?" he questioned, putting his glasses to his face so he could see her.

"Yes?" She tucked a strand of auburn hair behind her ear.

With a follow-me flick of his fingers, the man got up from his chair and walked toward the back of the empty restaurant, through a door that led down to the basement.

Chapter 2

Vera looked around the restaurant. Of the few people who were there, none of them appeared to even acknowledge this man suddenly trespassing in the back of the establishment, in an area usually restricted.

For a split second, she thought about just leaving. In the other half of that split second, she contemplated getting a Manhattan at the bar. Instead, realizing she had nothing to lose, Vera ventured toward the back of the restaurant, following the strange man's path.

As she made her way down the basement steps, the décor gradually evolved from cliché bistro fare to sleek and sophisticated walls and tiles.

Where am I going?

At the bottom of the staircase, she looked around and found herself in an office lobby environment, with a comfy black couch and shiny desk area in which the back of a tall chair faced her.

"I'm Bruce Kitchen, by the way," said the mystery man, who seemed to reappear out of nowhere. "Let me just get some things before we get started." He disappeared down another hallway.

Vera took a seat on the couch, crossing her legs after sinking into the cushion.

The dense, black chairback spun around and revealed another man—this one younger and attractive. "Tall, dark, and handsome" came to mind, but Vera dismissed the notion for its lack of originality.

"He's kind of like Alice's white ferret or whatever, isn't he?" the second man asked, shuffling some paperwork. His tone had a touch of unnecessary resentment.

"Excuse me?" asked Vera.

"*Alice in Wonderland.* Alice followed that white ferret down the ferret hole."

"You mean rabbit."

"Right." He stopped to think about it. "You sure it wasn't a ferret?" He looked at her out of the corner of his eyes.

"Positive."

Bruce returned with nothing in his hands, making Vera wonder why he had left in the first place.

"Hi, there, Vera. I see you've met Cole." Bruce gestured to the man in the chair.

Cole, thought Vera. *A man who apparently was never read to as a child.*

"Won't you join me in this conference room?"

Vera was astounded by the layers and levels to this restaurant.

The conference room looked like any conference room you'd see in an office building but with a huge mural on the walls: big, fake windows overlooking a big, fake sunny city. The design was so realistic that Vera had to do a double take before taking a seat.

"Isn't it a beautiful day in the city, Vera?" Bruce asked with a chuckle.

"Sure."

"Things are not always what they seem. Remember that."

"OK."

Vera started to wonder whether this was where she was going to die.

"So what interested you in my ad?" he asked.

"I was drawn to the word *library* actually. Do you need someone to archive or catalog materials?"

"Oh no. Nothing like that. We need characters."

Vera waited for more explanation, but it never came.

"I'm sorry?" she questioned, hoping to gain some clarity.

"Loan Some is a company that loans out people for events—funerals, weddings, birthdays, you name it."

Suddenly this place started to make sense to Vera. Loaning out people. A roundabout way of saying what Julia Roberts was in *Pretty Woman*. Sure, Vera knew she had the red hair, curvy build, and frankly, the desperation, but she was not going to go down *that* rabbit hole—yet. Ask her again in a month.

"I think you have the wrong girl." She got up from the conference room seat.

"What's your favorite book?" Bruce asked.

Favorite book? Vera had to think.

"*Sense and Sensibility*," said Vera matter-of-factly.

Bruce chuckled, taking a handkerchief from his pocket and patting sweat from his forehead. Vera wasn't sure whether he was actually perspiring or just doing it for dramatic effect.

"Let me guess," he said. "You tell people your favorite book is something by Jane Austen, but it's really something else entirely. Like a sci-fi novel. Or *Fear of Flying*."

Vera's eyes lit up. He was right. She loved Erica Jong's *Fear of Flying* and considered it to be a literary masterpiece, in spite of its blunt, erotic nature. She had always been afraid to offend her colleagues, who were fans of more canon writers like Dickens, Kafka, and Woolf.

"How did you know that?"

"Because, like I said, things are not always what they seem."

"Well, I'm still not going to be one of your call girls."

This made Bruce chuckle even harder.

"You think that's what this is?"

"You said you loaned people out." She crossed her arms.

Bruce stood up from the conference table and dimmed the lights, as if he were readying the room for a presentation. Standing in the doorway, Vera watched as he pulled down a projector screen, which covered one of the many skyscrapers in the city on the wall.

Within moments, there was a photograph of a bride and groom on the screen.

"Do you remember the Corliss wedding that was a viral sensation from a few months ago?"

Vera thought about it for a second. She didn't really stay up to date on pop culture and other happenings.

Bruce continued. "The one with the couple that walked down the aisle via jet packs?"

"Oh, right." Vera recalled the wedding's headline next to the one about the president's State of the Union address.

"Pretty crazy event, huh? Hundreds in attendance. At last count, the video had one and a half million views on YouTube."

Bruce flicked through photos on the projector—people from every walk of life, looking like they were having a wonderful time.

"What if I told you that only twenty people RSVPed?" he continued.

The montage of photos ceased, and Bruce brought the lights back up.

"The couple contacted us. They knew they wanted to do the jet pack thing for their wedding, but if no one was there to see it, what's the point in getting married, right? So they contacted us, and we sent two hundred guests out there with smartphones to make this wedding go viral."

"You can't be serious," said Vera.

"They had the money, just no friends, so that's where we come in. We provided them with loaners."

"Actors?"

"Nope. Just regular people, there to be landscape. Of course, this is a grand example. Most people don't have the money the Corliss couple did, but we get called for everything from bar mitzvahs to anniversaries to funerals."

"That is grim." Vera frowned.

"But in a world where communication is more technology focused, people don't have as many real human connections anymore, which means business has been booming."

"How did this even get started?"

"I threw a disastrous Oscar party a few years back," said Bruce, emphasizing *disastrous* as if it were spelled with a *z*. "No one showed. I talked up that party for a month beforehand and felt like a fool. After a couple of white wine spritzers, my marketing guru brother, Chuck, and I came up with Loan Some. And the rest is history."

"Oscars?" questioned Vera, with her eyebrow quirked.

"I am a huge fan of the cinema. It's my Super Bowl."

For some reason, the Oscar story had made this whole thing seem more legit to Vera. In her head she quickly weighed her options, like some sort of mental casino game. Instead of "cherry cherry cherry," she saw "zippity zippity doo dah." After mulling this over in the doorway, she retook her seat at the conference table.

"OK. So where do we go from here? Will there be a second round of interviews?"

"Nope. You're hired."

"That's it?"

"This isn't an easy gig," he said, using a tone Vera frequently used on loud patrons at the library. "We get a lot of nos, believe it or not."

"You have a way of making a gal feel wanted."

"Ground rules." Bruce reached under the conference table and pulled out a thick packet of pages for Vera, throwing it down on the table in front of her.

He continued. "You use a new name at each event. You have to change your appearance in some way for each hire. And you cannot, repeat, *cannot* make friends and/or romantic acquaintances with any of the guests."

"OK." Vera found it ironic that she was allowed to be fake friends with people that had no friends.

"And should your job be terminated, we don't know each other anymore, for confidentiality's sake. If this got out in the media, it would actually be disastrous for business."

"So why did you reveal the company's secret to me before I agreed to do it?"

"Because I knew you were going to take the job." His lips made a flat, Mona Lisa–esque line that told Vera he saw something special in her. She felt a twinge of excitement with the realization she was getting to live out her dream of being different characters like those in a book. This job was mysterious, something not even Ian Fleming would dream up.

"Pay works in this way," said Bruce. "We pay you a flat rate per hour, as mentioned in that packet. But if you do an outstanding job at an event, as deemed by the people that hire you, they can tip you."

Vera perused the packet as he talked. "How do I do an outstanding job?"

"Depends on the people. Sometimes you're hired just to be a number. Other times you may be hired to be the life of the party."

Bruce clapped his hands in an excited way, as if he were getting a football team riled up. "Ready for your first assignment?"

Chapter 3

*V*era took a deep breath and waited for Bruce to reveal what kind of adventure she'd be getting herself into.

"You're going to be a girlfriend at a comic book convention," he said. "If you'll look in that packet I handed you, you'll see the client."

Vera shuffled through the pages to see a picture of a man named Chip Killingsworth. He looked harmless enough—a nice smile and tousled, sandy-colored hair. Vera was suddenly flattered that she would be his fake girlfriend at an event. She'd never been arm candy before.

"He needs someone to be Chewbacca, and you fit the bill perfectly."

Vera looked up. "Excuse me?"

"Chewbacca. From *Star Wars*. You're pretty tall, and that's what he's looking for. He's going to be Yoda."

Vera's shoulders fell with a lilt.

The Chewbacca suit actually fit perfectly. There was something about the fur of the costume that made Vera feel warm and cozy, kind of like alpaca socks.

She was supposed to wait outside of the convention at the Civic Center—in full costume under Chip's stipulations. She felt like a bit of an idiot. Maybe this job wasn't as glamorous as she thought. James Bond wouldn't be caught in a *Star Wars* costume.

Hobbling up the convention center steps was a Yoda. In fact, hobbling up the convention center steps were *several* Yodas, which made discerning Chip from the others more difficult. Vera looked around from side to side before suddenly spotting a Yoda standing right next to her. Chip. He seemed to be two feet shorter than her.

"Isadora?"

"Yes. Hi, Chip." She held out a paw.

"Hot you do look."

Oh, right, thought Vera. *This backward-Yoda-speaking crap.* Vera wondered whether she should break it to Chip that she'd never actually seen the movies.

In response, Vera made a growl in an attempt to capture the essence of Chewbacca. Chip's elated smile faded, like the scroll in the signature opening sequence of the George Lucas film.

"We, shall?" Chip extended his arm, the one that didn't hold the lightsaber.

Inside, the convention kind of reminded her of *The Muppet Show* from when she was a child. Everyone was in costume, and there was every kind of person imaginable, kind of like a patch-work quilt of people.

"Hold my hand you will?" asked Yoda.

"Old this isn't getting," Vera muttered.

"Excuse me?"

Vera let out an anemic Chewbacca growl.

She held his hand as they walked at a pace that would be deemed slow at a nursing home. As they walked around, Vera noticed that many men and women were in elaborate costumes, some in beautiful gowns looking like characters that popped right out of a graphic novel. They were stunning.

"Would you like me to take off my head?" If Vera was going to be a girlfriend, she might as well sell it. She had put on some makeup that day to gussy herself up a bit.

Chip's Yoda ears twitched as he shot her a death stare.

"Ooookay," Vera said.

Since she was looking down at Chip, Vera wasn't paying attention and ran into someone—well, gingerly walked into someone, since they were moving at a glacial pace.

It was Cole, the hot guy from her initial interview at Loan Some. He was alone and dressed in an ensemble straight out of J.Crew. Vera suddenly felt grateful she was incognito.

"Sorry," she muttered, keeping her head down. As if he'd even recognize her amid all of the cognac-colored fur.

"No problem, *Isadora*," Cole muttered back before heading toward the *The Lord of the Rings* section, which featured a slew of different Frodos manning the area.

Isadora! Has he been tracking me?

"Excuse me will you?" asked Chip. "Calls, nature." He headed toward the restroom area, which was clear across the other side of the center. At the rate he was walking, she expected him to be back in time for the next *Star Wars* movie installment.

Vera wandered over to the *The Lord of the Rings* area, wondering if the literary ignoramus knew the Tolkien series only from the movies.

She purposefully bumped her furry shoulder against Cole's.

He looked up with a sly smile. "Hi, Chewie."

"Didn't peg you as a comic book fan."

"From the one conversation we ever had?"

"*Alice in Wonderland* went down a ferret hole?"

He looked left to right, making sure no one was watching them.

"We shouldn't even be talking," he said. "I'm just here to monitor you. Uncle Bruce sent me."

Uncle? "Bruce Kitchen is your uncle?"

"Yeah," he continued. "My dad helped start the company a few years back, after Uncle Bruce's disastrous Oscar party. He passed away last year, so I kind of took over his role."

Cole paused his story, his mouth gaping open, as a male Princess Leia walked past him, dressed in a bikini with his hairy stomach spilling out.

"Reluctantly," he said. He shook his head, as if to shake off the image. "You're doing fine, so far. We just want to make sure you don't have any issues with this first assignment."

"Thanks, I guess." So much for a vote of confidence. Vera doubted James Bond ever had any backup following him around. Then she stopped to question why she kept comparing herself to James Bond—why were there no literary female equivalents?

Soon, Vera noticed that the *The Lord of the Rings* table was rather empty. All of the Frodos were gone. She spun around. *Game of Thrones. The Avengers. Spiderman.* All of these areas were rather depleted of people too.

The roar of a crowd started to build, directing Vera's attention to the center of the convention center, where a mob had congregated. She and Cole looked at each other ominously—although she realized she was Chewie looking at Cole ominously—before venturing toward the crowd.

Because Vera was already tall, and the padding in the feet of the Chewie costume gave her a one-and-a-half-inch lift, she had a perfect view of what was causing the commotion.

Chapter 4

Chip, as Yoda, had somehow engaged in a lightsaber battle with *another* Yoda. Spectators had formed a circle around them, allowing the two Grand Masters of the Jedi Order enough space for their battle—over what, Vera didn't know.

"What happened?" she muttered to a Wonder Woman, whose iPhone was recording the duel.

"Nothing," Wonder Woman said. "They just saw each other and threw down immediately." Then she turned to Vera, realizing that Vera was dressed in *Star Wars* garb. "Chewie."

Because Chip's lightsaber was pretty remedial, something he clearly had created in high school out of wrapping paper tubes, he performed his own lightsaber sounds to make it more authentic. *Zhoom.* Meanwhile, the other Yoda clearly had spent a lot of time and money on his outfit and lightsaber, which made its own sounds when used. Yoda 2's entire outfit looked like it was issued straight from George Lucas himself.

Chip was clearly getting beat by this other guy, and the crowd was rallying behind Yoda 2 to finish him off.

"Should I do something?" Vera asked Cole.

"No. This will be over soon enough." He turned and walked away.

Just then Chip's lightsaber bent in half, reminiscent of Charlie Brown's sad Christmas tree. Knowing he had been beat, Chip brought his forlorn lightsaber to the front of his face, in the same way Obi-Wan did when he was defeated by Darth Vader in the first film, and the other Yoda fake-sliced his lightsaber across Chip's body. The crowd cheered and quickly rushed to Yoda 2, lifting him up and carrying him around.

After the audience had dispersed and gone back to what they were doing, Vera approached Chip, who was solemn.

"You put up a good fight," she said to Chip, playfully punching his shoulder. As she looked at him, with his Yoda ear bent from the battle, she felt a bit of pity.

"A Jedi uses the Force for knowledge and defense, never for attack."

"But you clearly just fought him, didn't you?"

"Patience you must have." Chip was really making her work for this assignment. She started to walk away, when he tugged on her fur costume. "Carry me will you?"

"Pardon?"

"Carry me."

Vera eyed him up and down. Given his small size, it was definitely doable. But did she really want to do this to herself? Being in a Chewie costume was humiliating enough.

Chip pulled out his fake, seafoam plastic hand and brushed his fingers back and forth in the same way a mob boss would ask, "Where's my dough?" Vera knew he would pay her extra if she did this.

"Hop on," she said.

He jumped on her back, and it was awkward as she took dinosaur steps, one at a time. He was heavier than she thought, and he ended up looking like a heavy backpack sliding off her shoulders.

She felt something hard against her back, and when she realized it wasn't his lightsaber, which had been discarded on the ground, she threw him off her shoulders.

"What the hell, Chip?" said a woman dressed as Hermione from *Harry Potter.*

Chip was rolling around on the floor like some sort of dying ant. "Hi, Alexis," he said. "This is Isadora."

"Hello, Isadora," said Alexis. "I'm Chip's wife."

Vera, as Chewie, shot Chip a look. Chip got up from his dead-ant-like position, straightening his Jedi robe and adjusting his ears.

Oh, God, Vera thought. *Am I a fake home wrecker?* She had never imagined that the person that hired her would be a phony too.

"Are you going to explain?" asked Alexis, with her hands on her hips.

"Understand you gotta—"

"In non-Jedi speak," Alexis interrupted.

"We have been growing apart," he said in a fairly normal voice, even if he still tended to sound like something from Jim Henson's Creature Shop. "You never even look at me anymore. You're so invested in books. And when the *Divergent* book series came out, well, crap. I knew I'd never see you anymore."

"I only got interested in the book series because of you." Tears swelled up in her eyes. "I know you've been playing again. I found Settlers of Catan hidden behind the toilet."

Chip winced, embarrassed by this revelation.

Vera couldn't follow half of what either one of them was saying.

"I'm sorry, Lexie." He paused, collecting his thoughts so he wouldn't get too emotional. "I'll get help. I only brought Isadora here to try to make you jealous. She's no one to me."

And maybe it was hearing it out loud, but suddenly Vera realized why some people were so apt to quit this job.

Yoda and Hermione hugged, and then started to make out. Vera turned her head away and shut her eyes.

"You know," said Alexis, "I do approve of *some* role-playing games."

"OK," said Vera. "That's enough."

They both turned to her, with looks as if to say, "You're still here?" Yoda pulled away from Alexis to speak with Isadora privately.

"I guess you're off the hook for the rest of your services today," he said. "I'll pay you in full. We'll be in touch."

He started to walk away, when Vera gave him a big ol' tap on his shoulder. Chip turned around to see Chewbacca staring him down and making the "Where's my money?" mobster gesture with her Muppet hands.

"Fine," he said. "I'll tip you, too."

As Yoda and Hermione walked away, Vera felt like she had actually done something good with her job: bringing a couple on the brink of divorce back together. She'd never done this at the library.

She decided to take off her Chewie helmet and breathe a little, and just as she felt the cool air hit her face, Cole was back.

"You know you can't do that," he said. "You're supposed to remain in your role until specified."

"Relax," she said. "He doesn't need my services anymore. He's reunited with his wife."

"Yoda's married?" Cole's face scrunched in a mixture of disgust and morbid curiosity.

"Yes, and thanks to me, he's reunited with his estranged spouse."

"Well, good for you. But you still better put that Chewie head back on. You could run into someone you know."

As Cole and Vera walked toward the exit of the convention, Vera stopped dead in her tracks when she encountered a blast from her not-too-distant past.

Chapter 5

$\mathcal{J}$effrey actually looked spruced up for the comic convention. No ratty T-shirt or sweatpants here. In fact, he looked more decked out for this than he had for any of their dates. Probably because he was with another girl. As Vera processed this, she also realized *she* wasn't supposed to be there—Isadora was.

"Vera?" He tilted his head in a clueless, innocent kind of way that almost made her attracted to him again. But before Jeffrey was able to recognize his former flame, Cole grabbed Vera and kissed her, dipping her as if they were dancing. Jeffrey and his date, a woman wearing a shirt with an embroidered cat on it, gawked for a moment.

"I thought Chewie was my ex," he said to the woman as they walked away. "She'd never be caught dead here though." They moved on to the superhero exhibit.

Cole's lips felt soft and sweet to Vera. As they were making out, the word *delicious* popped into her brain for some reason—one of her most favorite words of all time. While he was kissing her, Cole kept one eye on Jeffrey to see if he had left. Once he realized

Jeffrey was no longer there, he dropped Vera with a thump, like Chewbacca roadkill.

"Ouch," said Vera. "What was that for?"

"To teach you a lesson," he said. "Follow the rules."

"No," she said, getting up and dusting herself off, "I know why you dropped me, but why did you kiss me? We could have just lied our way out of that situation. It's not like I was with Chip."

"When it comes to people you know, or have some sort of history with, it can be hard to lie to them. They know you. They'll see right through you." He pulled a piece of debris out of Vera's hair and smoothed it. "And I can tell you right now that you were going to come up with an awful set of lies that would incriminate you."

"I had it covered," she said.

He raised his eyebrows at her as they continued to walk toward the exit.

"So what do we do now?"

"You're going to have to check in with Uncle Bruce after the assignment. Your payment should be processed ASAP, granted that Chip is on time."

Outside of the convention center, comic book and sci-fi fans were still piling in as Vera and Cole were filing out. It was a sunny day, with the blue sky beckoning people to be out enjoying the weather. It made Vera sad that so many people were headed indoors. This kind of weather always made her want to find a good book and a shady tree.

"So what are you up to the rest of the day?" she asked as they walked toward their cars. Vera had to admit that she couldn't get her mind off that kiss.

Just then, a short, petite blond woman walking toward them threw her arms around Cole's shoulders.

"Hey, honey," she said to Cole. "I tried calling you. You off work yet?"

He kissed her politely while still looking at Vera, as if this were awkward for him. "Jill," he said, pulling away from her, "this is Vera, Uncle Bruce's new hire."

Jill gave one look at Vera in her Chewie costume and let out a cutesy laugh.

Vera found herself standing by a black BMW and saw this as a way to excuse herself.

"Well, this is me," she said to Cole and Jill.

Cole's eyes bugged out when he noticed her car.

"A BMW? Nice ride."

"Thanks," she said, standing back and admiring the car. "But it's not mine. Mine's over there." She pointed at an old Chevy Cobalt across the street.

He looked at her curiously.

"See?" she said. "I, too, can lie."

She left them behind her like two heroes riding off into the sunset. Of course he would have a girlfriend. Why wouldn't he?

As she crossed the street, two men wearing a cardboard *Star Trek Enterprise* outfit, like two children dressed in a horse costume on Halloween, came running down the street, crashing right into Vera. However, the costume was so weak, as were the men, that they quite literally bounced right off of Vera, falling to the ground.

"Are you guys all right?" she asked, throwing her Chewbacca head on the ground so she could help them up.

"Yeah," said one guy, dressed as Spock. She gave him her hand, and when he pulled himself up, his head reached her shoulders. Vera sighed. Yet another man that she towered over in height.

"We actually were trying to track you down," said the other guy, dressed as Captain Kirk, who had managed to get himself back on his feet.

"Me? You were trying to track me down?" Vera suddenly grew worried that she had done something horribly wrong back at the convention. Was she supposed to genuflect by the Captain America section on the way out?

"We're Chip's friends," said Spock. "We know what you did."

"I carried him on my back because he needed help," she said. "That's not something I normally do."

"No, not that," said Kirk. "We know he hired you to be his girl-friend today."

"Oh."

"I was wondering if you were available for a wedding in a few weeks," said Spock. "My ex-girlfriend's going to be there, and it would be great if I could have you on my arm."

"I'm having a Halloween party, and I think it's going to be a dude fest," said Kirk. "What are you doing at the end of the month?"

Vera was overwhelmed. Bruce Kitchen was right. Business was booming.

"I don't have a business card on me right now," said Vera, "but you can reach me at this number. Can I put my number in your cell phone?"

"Sure." Spock handed her his phone, and Vera attempted punching the numbers with her furry Chewbacca hands. She ended up pressing multiple numbers at once.

"On the other hand," said Vera, "why don't I just tell you my number?"

After she gave them her number, they went on their way.

"Live, prosper," she said as they headed toward the convention.

They turned around and grimaced at her pop culture faux pas.

Vera got into her car and eventually found herself back at Market Street Place, Loan Some's headquarters.

As she was walking down the basement steps, another woman was walking up them at the same time. She was dressed in a black skirt suit. They looked each other up and down curiously, acknowledging that they both had been on assignments.

"Funeral," the woman said, signaling to her attire.

"Comic book convention," Vera replied, signaling to hers.

In the basement, Bruce Kitchen was waiting for her. "How'd it go?" he asked.

"Good," said Vera. "Really good, actually."

"Chip submitted payment. Here's your first paycheck." Bruce handed it to her with a warm smile. "Great to have you aboard."

Vera looked at the piece of paper in front of her. As happy as she was to be able to pay rent on time this month, she had another feeling that was new to her. For the first time in her life, nothing was organized. If she were going to give this chapter of her life a library section, she'd probably file it under *miscellaneous*. She had no idea what would happen tomorrow, yet she couldn't wait for morning.

PART II:

"Eventually these two different lives intersect."

Chapter 6

*V*era looked around the housewarming party and saw friends who were supposed to be strangers.

Phill Conrad, a fellow Loan Some hire that frequently reminded people there were two *l*'s in his name, was there. Today he was dressed in a sweater-vest and was going by the alias Bradley Bradwell. Then there was Gabi Vega, married mother of two and Loan Some hire of nearly two years. Today she was going by Margo Curran and was posing as Bradley Bradwell's hotsy-totsy girlfriend, clad in a skintight black dress.

In the months since Vera had started working at Loan Some, she had been on plenty of assignments—funerals, bar mitzvahs, baby showers, just to name a few. During one gig, she was hired to simply sit in the open gallery area of a trial, just to look like the defendant had a friend that cared about her during a case about a broken lease. (Vera was hired by the lawyer, not the defendant.) However, of all the assignments she had been on in recent weeks, this one was proving to be the most fun. It was almost like an office party, with all of the loaners getting a chance to actually talk to each other, since the party consisted mostly of people hired to look like they were friends with Dutch Skoblow, the party thrower.

Wearing a Liza Minelli–esque wig while sipping some champagne in a corner, Vera chatted with fellow loaner Maudie Meisel, as she tugged at her wig to make sure her red tendrils didn't pop out.

"How long have you been with LS?" asked Maudie.

"Seven months or so. You?"

"Two years. Full-time. Used to be a travel agent." Maudie took a big swig of her drink.

"Librarian." Vera raised her hand in a guilty manner.

"Is this where extinct jobs go?"

Vera shrugged.

"I don't know what my end game is," said Maudie. "But I remodeled my kitchen. What are you hoping to get out of it?"

Vera wasn't really sure what she wanted just yet. For right now, she was just happy to be able to make rent and put food on the table.

"I'm sure being a fake partygoer wasn't what my parents envisioned for me." Vera thought about her years of schooling and how she was now being paid to be a prostitute of friendship.

"What do they do?"

"Dad's a real estate agent, and Joe's a teacher." Vera hated talking about her fathers, not because she didn't love them but because she was never sure what kind of reaction she was going to get from bystanders.

Maudie smiled. "Raised by two dads? That's awesome."

"I imagine it's probably not much different than being raised by a man and woman. Still got in trouble for the same things most kids get in trouble for. Like staying up past midnight to finish a book."

"Nerd," said Maudie, her eyes bugging out a little when she said it. "So I take it 'Dad' is your birth father? Where's Mom?"

Vera paused before responding. A good question. "My mother and father had me when they were pretty young, and after she gave birth, she just…left."

"Wow. You ever think of trying to find her?"

Vera thought about the Google searches and slow nights at the library spent combing through old newspaper clippings. She had just wanted to find out what her mother ended up doing. She didn't necessarily want to connect with her and spend evenings braiding each other's hair. She just wanted to let her know that Dad and Joe had done a good job. Ultimately, she wanted her to see that the baby girl she left behind had become a woman.

Before Vera could answer, Dutch rang his wine glass with a fork to make an announcement. "Hello, everyone. Thank you for coming to my party. I'd like to get a picture of everyone together to put on Facebook." Dutch had a Santa Claus quality about him, his cheeks jolly red and his tummy out and proud.

Maudie rolled her eyes so only Vera could see her do it. "The dream of being popular on Facebook is what keeps this company in business," she whispered.

The group congregated together for the photo, a ragtag team of loaners and real people whom Dutch would tag as friends on Facebook, when really he knew maybe 5 percent of them. In fact, the photo ended up being a great Loan Some company pic.

As the photo group (and party) dispersed, Vera noticed a hand-some nonloaner looking at her in an interested but not creepy way. He had kind brown eyes, which actually drew her in beyond every-thing else—even if everything else looked *pretty* good. Vera knew the rule: do not date the "real" people at these parties. So she tried to break eye contact and get on her merry way.

As Vera was leaving Dutch's housewarming party, gathering her coat and purse at the door, she felt the touch of a hand at her arm. She turned around to see the nonloaner hottie she had made eye contact with.

"Hi," he said. "My name's Greg Goodman. I didn't get a chance to introduce myself." He put out his hand. Vera tried not to eye him up and down, but he was too cute, with an effortlessly chic look about him. Classic but casual trousers, a collared shirt with a hoodie over it, and then a jean jacket to cap it all off.

Vera tugged at her wig to make sure it was still in place. She almost responded with her real name but then recalled the Loan Some rules: do not date anyone at these events, and do not give them your real name.

"Louisa Gradgrind." She shook his hand.

"How do you know Dutch?"

"We used to work together. How do you know him?"

"Neighbor down the street. I wasn't planning on staying long, but it ended up being a nice party."

"It did." She really wanted to stay and chat longer, but she could feel her interest in him growing, so she decided to just cut it off there. "Well, I have to go. It was nice meeting you."

"Here's my card," he said, pulling a cardboard square out of his jacket pocket and handing it to her.

Vera's eyes went agog when she read his card: *Greg Goodman, Executive Vice President, Chief Marketing and Sales Officer, Tenley E-books*. "E-books?" She grimaced. "I don't think so." She handed the card back to him.

"You don't like e-books?"

"No way. They put me out of business."

"What business were you in?"

"I used to be a librarian."

"And now?"

Vera stopped herself. "I've already said too much. I've got to go."

She exited the house, and he followed behind her. "At least tell me your name then."

"I already told you. Louisa Gradgrind."

"I mean your real name."

His words stopped her in her tracks. She turned around to face him, careful to make sure none of the other loaners were around to spot how he had outed her. Luckily, they were alone. He walked slowly toward her, shortening the distance between them so that eventually they were face-to-face.

"Here," he said, flipping the card between his fingers while donning a polite, schoolboy smirk.

Back at her apartment, Vera placed Greg's card on the desk in her bedroom. Then she plopped herself down on the bed, eyeing the phone on her nightstand, before picking it up, dialing a number, and twirling her fingers around the cord as she waited for a response.

"Vera!" said a man's voice on the other end. "Honey, where've you been?"

"Sorry. I know. I've been busy."

"When are you going to tell us about this new job? We want details."

"I'll have to explain it in person, but I can tell you it's going well."

"OK." He said this as though trying to use guilt to make her tell him more about the job. It didn't work.

"I have a question, though."

"Shoot, kid."

"What do you really know about Mom?"

There was silence on the other end.

"Dad?"

"I mean, it's been thirty-some years. You were a baby."

"Do you have any idea what her whereabouts are nowadays?"

"Honey, is something wrong?"

Vera could see she was making her father uncomfortable, so she changed the subject. "I was just wondering. Anyway, how's Joe?"

Bleep.

Vera noticed another call was coming through her phone. It was from Loan Some, according to the caller ID.

"Actually, Dad, can I call you back? I have a work call coming through the call waiting."

"Call waiting? What year this is?"

"Love you. I'll call you back in a second." Vera didn't want to argue with him yet again about why she should use her cell phone more often and come into the twenty-first century.

Chapter 7

Vera answered the other line on the call waiting. "Hello?"

"Vera, it's Cole."

For the red-haired former librarian, his deep voice conjured up images of their shared kiss at the comic book convention. Ever since that day, they had shared only brief encounters, like run-ins at headquarters, but nothing substantial. In fact, this phone conversation was already the most words they had shared in months.

"We need you down at headquarters," he continued. "Uncle Bruce has a new assignment for you."

"Anything you can tell me about over the phone?"

"Do you think I'd be calling you to come down to headquarters if I could do this over the phone?"

She remembered why they didn't talk much. She kind of hated him.

The funny thing about Loan Some's headquarters was that none of the restaurant patrons or staff ever seemed to wonder what went on in the basement. For each assignment, Vera would enter Market Street Place, waving to the bartender as she passed the bar area before venturing down the back steps to the basement area that was the Loan Some office, and no one would ever question her.

Today, Cole greeted her at the front desk. "Finally," he chided.

"I left as soon as I hung up with you."

His blond, petite girlfriend came out of the bathroom in click-clocky heels that announced her entrance.

"Hi, Vera," she said.

"Jill."

And that was it. They stood there, staring at each other like idiots. Vera hadn't liked the way Jill mocked her with silent condescension when she was dressed as Chewbacca. From what Vera gathered through overheard cell phone conversations, Jill was a physical trainer that enjoyed Katherine Heigl movies. Vera wasn't even sure what a Katherine Heigl was.

"Well," said Cole, "I hate to break up this conversation, but Uncle Bruce wants you in the conference room."

Vera smiled at Jill and Cole, as some sort of awkward segue, and headed into the conference room. When Vera entered the room, Bruce was at the conference table, shuffling papers and folders. She swore he did this just for effect sometimes.

"Vera," he said. "Good to see you. Shut the door and sit down."

Vera did as he directed. "What's going on, Bruce?"

"Big assignment. We want you to be in on it." Bruce handed her a folder. "Have you heard of this guy?"

Vera opened the folder to see a photo of a man around her age, wearing a black suit. Attractive. Name: Owen Staley.

"No," she said. "Should I know him?"

"Owen was on a matchmaking show for millionaires. However, they couldn't find him a match. Somehow he learned about us and wants to hire someone to take to a family wedding. For an entire week."

"Any idea how he heard about us?"

"I suspect one of our former loaners now works for him at his tech company."

Vera flipped through the folder to read more about this Owen Staley character. He came from an affluent family. Parents Elizabeth and Richard Staley. Even if he came from money, he had made even more creating a tech company that specialized in how to avoid vehicular traffic.

Upon closer examination of his picture, Vera discovered he had freckles, almost as if he were a redhead. Yet his hair was black. She wondered whether he dyed his hair to avoid being a redhead, which she found offensive since *she* was a redhead. Plus, redheads were going extinct, according to a *National Geographic* article that Vera had perused before the library closed. Redheads were a rare breed, like dinosaurs, that needed to be preserved and celebrated.

But before Vera could get worked up over the redhead debate, she took a look at what Mr. Staley was willing to pay for Loan Some's services. She did a double take. Maudie Meisel could redo five of her kitchens with this money.

"That's a big payout," she said, flicking the folder closed.

"So you wanna do it?"

Of course she wanted to do it. She was never one to have money on the brain, but for some reason, she envisioned buying a house and getting out of her crummy, one-bedroom apartment.

"Absolutely."

"There's one catch," said Bruce, removing his eyeglasses from his face so that they dangled around his neck from their chain.

Vera raised her eyebrows in anticipation.

"He's a total asshole, pardon my French."

"What?"

"It's why they couldn't find him a date and probably why he's still single. He's extremely difficult. However, he's willing to pay big."

"How bad can he be?" Vera shrugged. "After all, I was a loaner for that guy who ate nothing but garlic."

"That's why we knew you'd be perfect for this assignment."

Vera had dealt with plenty of assholes in her life. Frat boys that never shut up in the reference section. Old people that screamed at her because they owed twenty-five cents on an overdue book. She was confident she could handle some washed-up reality show star that couldn't find love or even a warm body to take to his family's wedding.

As Vera was leaving the Loan Some office, Cole followed her out.

"Where's Jill?" she asked. "Is there a *Real Housewives* training course she had to be at?"

Cole smirked. "Given how little you know of pop culture, I appreciate that you had to work for that slam."

They walked up the basement steps in unison.

"So I was thinking we could drive together to the wedding," he said.

"Excuse me?" Vera stopped in her tracks. "You're coming with me?"

"This guy's brutal, Vera. We want everything going to plan and nothing ending up in the tabloids."

"What's so awful about this guy?"

Cole made a *sheesh* gesture with his mouth. "Where to start?" he said. "Let me pull up a clip on my phone."

Cole pulled out his phone, and his thumbs quickly found a clip from YouTube.

"Your phone has video? Cool."

Cole gave a sore side-glance to Vera for her remedial knowledge of modern technology.

"Here it is," he said.

Vera watched as Owen sat across from a beautiful blonde in what looked like the living room of a mansion. "Leslie," he said soberly, almost as if he were putting on a performance, "I'd like you to accept this necklace as a token of my affection on one condition."

"Yes," said Leslie, who was wiping away tears. "Of course. What?"

"I'd really like you to get a boob job."

The camera panned to Leslie's face, which had a flash of utter devastation, as if he had run over a litter of puppies with his car or, you know, told a woman he'd only date her if she received breast enhancements.

After the clip ended, Cole put the phone back into his pocket.

"I'm spending a week with a guy like that?" Vera's neck jutted out like an angry bobblehead doll before her eyes fell to subtly examine the worthiness of her own curvy body. "He may not want me."

"Relax," said Cole. "He chose you from among the loaners he looked at."

"Really? I thought you and Bruce chose me for the assignment."

"It was a combination of both."

Eventually, she and Cole found themselves outside of the building. It was a brisk spring evening, and restaurant-goers were starting to venture into Market Street Place.

"Anyway," said Cole, "I'll be on hand if you need me."

"Well, thanks," she said, although it made her just as nervous to know Cole was involved now.

There was an awkward moment of silence as cute couples, unlike themselves, ventured into the restaurant for date night.

"Do you wanna get a cup of coffee?" he asked.

Vera was surprised he was so brazen all of the sudden. He never appeared to so much as want to recognize her in the street outside of work. Now he was asking her to coffee?

"Sure," said Vera.

"Cool. I'm waiting for Jill to get outta work. She has a late physical training consulting thingy tonight."

"Uh-huh." Vera hated when people used her to bide their time between people that were more important.

At Kafka Café, Vera sipped black tea with milk while Cole drank black coffee.

"So what do you do?" he asked.

"Excuse me?"

"You know. Outside of work. What gets you going?"

Vera raised her eyebrows.

"In a nonsexual way, perv," he said before taking a sip from his white ceramic mug.

"I don't know. I like to read. Go to city events."

"No guy?"

Vera found it adorable the way his eyes got boyishly curious as he took another sip.

"No. Not right now."

And just as she said "now," Greg Goodman walked into the café, stopping to pick up a newspaper at a stand by the counter.

Chapter 8

Cole noticed Vera staring at the man at the counter.

"Who's that?" Cole sounded almost pouty.

"No one." Vera drew her head down, with her hand over her face, her eyes peeking through her fingers. If Cole found out she had connected with someone at a party as a loaner, she could be in major trouble.

Cole raised his eyebrows at *her* this time.

Despite her efforts to go unnoticed, Greg had discovered her and sauntered over to their café table.

"Thought that was you," he said. "Your hair looks different." Then he sized up his competition in Cole. "I'm Greg." He put out his hand.

"Cole." They shook hands.

"Cole's my coworker," said Vera. As much as she didn't want Greg to come over to their table, she also didn't want him to think she was *with* Cole.

"What is it that you do again, Louisa?" asked Greg. "You never told me."

Cole gave Vera a suspicious stare.

"I work in loans. It's boring. So hey," said Vera, attempting to change the subject, "have you had the orange-cream coffee cake here? It's amazing."

"What is it that you do?" said Cole.

"I work in e-books."

"People are still reading?"

"Yes. Lots of people are reading. In fact, the advent of the e-book is like the modern-day equivalent of the printing press. Educating the masses."

"I cheerfully disagree," chimed in Vera.

"Cheerfully?" Greg smiled. "I've never been cheerfully disagreed with before."

Vera and Greg stared at each other for a few moments, with looks of innocent flirtation. Despite his working in e-books, something she detested, she liked him. There was just an ease about him.

"You know what they haven't figured out yet?" asked Cole, disrupting the flow between Vera and Greg. "Wrapping paper. So much waste. Why purchase something just to throw it away? Are you guys working on e-wrapping paper yet?"

Greg gave him a polite but annoyed expression. "No. Not yet." He looked back at Vera. "So I'm gonna let you guys get back to… this. Nice seeing you, Louisa."

Greg went back to the line to order coffee.

"I'm going to pretend that this never happened," said Cole.

"I know."

"You know the rules."

"But he's kind of yummy."

"Please. E-books. Come on."

"Well, I'm with you on that one."

Just then, Cole's cell phone began to ring. "I'm gonna take this. It's Jill." Cole went outside to take the call.

It looked like Greg had sneaked out.

A female barista came over to Vera's table and handed her a note.

"This is for you," she said. "From Greg."

Vera read the note: "I'll be here again tomorrow at 7 p.m. I hope to see you here. Alone."

Obviously, Greg and Cole had not hit it off.

Just then, Cole came back into the café, slipping his phone into his back pocket. "I have to go," he said. "Jill's done with work." Cole eyed the note in Vera's hand. "What'd I miss?"

"Nothing," said Vera, folding it and putting it into her pocket. "One of the patrons here passed me a note saying you were entirely too obnoxious on the phone."

"Are you kidding? I excused myself outside."

Vera shrugged.

Then, upon realizing she was lying, he gave Vera a disgusted look. "So while I was outside, I got a call from Uncle Bruce. We're leaving tomorrow night for the wedding."

"Tomorrow night?"

"Yeah. Is that a problem?"

"No."

"I'm gonna jet. Let's meet at headquarters tomorrow around eight."

After Cole left, Vera unfolded the note the barista had handed to her and looked it over. Even Greg's handwriting was enticing. It had been so long since she'd been in a real relationship with an adult male. Jeffrey was the last in a line of infantile suitors. She wasn't going down that road again.

Back at her apartment, with a suitcase open on her bed, Vera packed for this long workweek ahead, tossing in dresses and fancy attire for the wedding. Well, dresses from T.J.Maxx. As she packed, she started to grow more curious about this millionaire matchmaker, so she got on her laptop and Googled "Owen Staley." Google autocompleted his name with "is an asshole." Not a good sign.

After learning more about Owen via tabloid images and Wikipedia, she got the itch to once again try the same thing with her mother's name.

She had tried it years before, taking out a Facebook account solely to find her mother. However, she was never able to find anything on her, and after growing annoyed with people's updates about cats and empty political statements, she deactivated her account.

Maybe this time would be different. She reactivated her Facebook account and hoped for the best, typing "Betsey Burrows" into the search bar.

This time, among the many Betsey Burrows that came up, a profile with a face that looked strangely familiar appeared. Vera clicked on it, but since the profile was private, she was able to see only the image and no other info on this particular Betsey Burrows.

The woman appeared to be around the age her mother would be and had red hair just like Vera. She was beautiful, which made Vera excited at the genetic prospect of aging like her. Despite having no proof, she somehow felt deep down inside that this woman had given birth to her so many years ago.

Just as she was about to click "Send Message" on Betsey Burrows's page, the phone on her nightstand rang. She ventured over to her dresser and picked it up gingerly. "Hello?"

"Thanks for calling me back," said her father. Despite the degree of sarcasm, it was comforting to hear his voice.

"Sorry. I got caught up with work." She looked at her alarm clock on her nightstand. It was after midnight. "Why are you calling me so late?"

"I can't sleep. And I just wanted to say something."

"What?"

Vera's father rarely ever used such a serious tone, so she knew that it had to be bad. Thoughts raced through her head. Cancer. A weird terminal illness. What was he going to tell her at 12:14 in the morning?

"Don't try to find your mother."

"Oh."

"I don't want you to be disappointed."

Vera digested his statement before responding. "OK."

"I love you, Vera."

"Love you too, Dad."

Then he hung up.

Vera looked back at the Facebook screen with her possible mother's image staring back at her. As much as Vera didn't want to abandon her desire to learn more about her mother, she also didn't want to betray her father's wishes, so she simply closed out of the Facebook page of the lovely redhead who may or may not have given birth to her so many years ago.

Chapter 9

Around six the next evening, Vera found herself packed and ready to go for this assignment. She had hoped she would procrastinate and time would run over, bleeding into that seven o'clock time slot Greg had given her, but she definitely had enough space to stop by and see Greg, if he was even there.

At 7:00 p.m. sharp, Vera found herself at Kafka Café, lugging her travel drag bag behind her. She looked around the coffee shop. An old couple drinking tea in the corner, a teenager and friends on their cell phones, and a businessman on his laptop. *Good*, she thought. As much as she wanted to see Greg, she secretly hoped he wouldn't show, so her life wouldn't get any more complicated.

She ordered an espresso and sat down at a table, figuring this would be a good time to catch up on rereading *The Corrections*.

Just then Greg walked in, purchased a coffee at the counter, and plopped his stuff down in the seat across from her.

"You came," he said.

"I did."

"Didn't think you would."

"I didn't think I would either."

He scooted his seat closer to the table so he could be closer to her.

"Now will you give me a name? I know Louisa Gradgrind is a Dickens character. You think I don't know books because I'm in e-books?"

"Vera. My name is Vera."

"Nice to meet you, Vera." He eyed the drag bag next to her. "Where you off to?"

"Business."

"Perfect. That leads to my second question. What is it that you do with loans?"

"I'm a loan officer. I have to assess this business proposal out of town."

"Fair enough. Where out of town?"

"Newport, Rhode Island." This part was true. The wedding was going to be ritzy. After all, she was going with a millionaire.

"I'm really getting you to spill secrets now. So when do you get back?"

"In about a week. But what about you? I'm tired of talking about me."

"Divorced. No kids. Nonsmoker." He looked up toward the ceiling, searching for words. "I don't like bicyclists."

"Bicyclists?"

"They drive me crazy on the road. I'm always so worried about hitting them with my car."

They continued to chat, and Vera found herself really liking this guy—so much so that she lost track of time. Cole coming into the café jolted her back into the reality that this was not a date but a pit stop before this big assignment. Spotting Vera and Greg sharing an intimate moment, Cole beelined it to their table after getting his coffee.

"Well," said Cole. "Nice seeing you here again, Greg."

"Same here."

And that was it. The two of them didn't say anything else, taking a swig of their coffees instead.

"Well," said Vera, "I hate to break up this conversation, but Cole and I should really get going."

"You're going to Newport with him?" said Greg.

"You told him we're going to Newport?" Cole looked like he wanted to throttle Vera.

"Yes, Cole. I didn't think it would be a big deal to tell him that we have to assess a loan there."

Vera stood up, gathering her things. Greg also stood up.

"It was lovely to see you, Greg."

"The pleasure was mine." He leaned into her and kissed her on the cheek. Vera tried not to blush as Cole looked on, tapping his watch apathetically.

As Cole and Vera exited the café, Vera looked behind at Greg, who was watching her as she left.

"Who's driving?" asked Vera.

"Oh. Change of plans."

With a look at what was parked in front of Kafka Café, Vera realized it was going to be an interesting trip.

"A limo?" she said.

"Owen Staley sent it for us." The limo driver, standing next to the vehicle, opened the door for Cole and Vera. Inside, the limo had bottled water, Kashi snacks, and champagne, among other assorted foods.

"I thought he was supposed to be a jerk," said Vera as she cracked open a bottle of water. She sniffed the water before taking a sip.

"Well, we are working for him," said Cole. "Maybe he felt the need to treat the hired help nicely."

"I want you to play back what you just said."

"Want to watch a movie?" Cole grabbed the remote to the TV in the limo and turned it on. "Look through those DVDs on the floor."

Within a box was everything from *Weekend at Bernie's* to *Annie Hall*. As Vera rummaged through it, the soft purr of the limo's engine started, and soon they were off on the road.

"Pick one," said Cole.

"I've never seen any of these."

"You're kidding."

"I like to read. I find that movies lack an omniscient presence."

"Let's watch *The Apartment*. I think you'll like it."

"What's it about?"

"In order to get ahead at his company, a guy offers his apartment as a way for his bosses to conduct affairs with women."

"Nice," Vera said steeped in sarcasm.

"I promise you'll like it."

He popped in the DVD, and the sweeping opening-credits music swelled as both he and Vera got comfortable in their limo seats.

"Is Jill OK with you being away this week?"

"Not really. I had to turn off my phone so she won't constantly text me for updates. Like, I'm in a limo. What else can I tell her right now?"

"Want a blanket? I brought one."

"Sure."

Vera opened a blanket from one of her bags and unfurled it for the both of them. Then they looked at each other with knowing smiles, almost as if they were little kids that got to sit at the adult table at Thanksgiving dinner. This assignment already had its perks.

Vera couldn't remember the last time she went to a movie theater or even watched a movie. But as she watched this Billy Wilder film, she couldn't help but feel a little like a villainess for identifying with Mr. Sheldrake, the man who cheats on his wife with Shirley MacLaine. Sure, she wasn't cheating on anyone, but in a way, she felt like she was cheating on life every time she posed as a friend for someone else or a mourner at a funeral. She was cheating people out of authentic human experience.

"This movie feels a little too close to home."

"How so?" Cole arched his eyebrow.

"I mean, in ways, I lead two different lives. My own, and then this loaner persona, whatever it is on a particular day."

"Well, keep watching."

"Why?"

"Because eventually these two different lives intersect."

Vera continued to watch the screen, but Cole could see that she was struggling with issues beyond what was on the monitor.

He paused the movie with a click of the remote. "Do you not like what you're doing here?" he said.

"I guess sometimes," she said, "I feel like I'm a loaner in my own life, substituting what I really want to do with being everyone else's stand-in. In some ways, Loan Some is just me stalling before I figure out what I'm actually going to do with my life."

"You mean you don't see yourself with the company forever?" he asked with sarcasm and a wink.

"It's a weird gig that I do enjoy. But at some point, I'm going to have to come up with a new game plan." She smiled weakly at him. "I'm sorry. I didn't mean to get emotional on you. And spill so much about how I feel about my job, when you're kind of my boss."

"It's OK. I feel the same way." He leaned his head back against the seat and sighed. "You think I like this? I lost my job as a marketing director in New York, and then I had to help take over this quirky family business. Not exactly ideal."

"Why don't you just get out of it? I'm sure Bruce would understand."

"I guess I feel some sort of obligation to him. And to the spirit of my father." He shot a look at Vera. "Well, you've certainly killed the vibe."

"Press play." She laughed.

Hours later, the door of the limo opened, allowing beautiful sunlight to pour through the vehicle. Vera discovered that *The Apartment* was on the main menu screen. She had fallen asleep before she could find out whether Fran Kubelik would recover from her suicide attempt. Vera also discovered that she was using Cole's body as a pillow, as her head was nestled against his shoulder. She pulled away right before he woke up.

"What's going on?" said Cole.

"I think we're here."

Vera climbed out of the limo, and Cole followed. They were welcomed by the stately Rosecliff Mansion looming over them, its white pillars standing tall like guards.

"This is where we're staying?" asked Cole.

"No," said a voice.

Vera turned to see Owen Staley coming out from behind one of the tall green bushes. "This is where the wedding is. Cole will be staying at the Cliffside Inn. But you—" Owen grabbed Vera's hand and kissed it. "You will be staying with me."

"Owen," said a female voice, "who's your lady friend?"

Vera turned her head to follow the voice and discovered a strangely familiar face. She couldn't quite pinpoint it at first until it dawned on her. The woman from Facebook—the one she thought was her mother! This woman was walking out of the mansion.

"This is—"

"Denise Lambert," said Vera, putting out her hand.

"Betsey," said the woman. As Vera shook Betsey's hand, she couldn't help but think, *Am I shaking my mother's hand?*

Betsey stopped to look her over. "Do I know you?"

Vera didn't know how *The Apartment* ended, but she suddenly understood the idea of two lives intersecting.

Chapter 10

"You look familiar." Betsey looked Vera up and down with her hand to her chest in polite surprise, as if she were clutching a set of pearls like a 1950s' housewife instead of what she was actually clutching—a diamond-encrusted necklace that was probably worth half a year's librarian salary. Vera also noted that Betsey's chest quickly rose in and out, indicating that this shock had left her out of breath.

Vera searched for words but froze. She wanted to say something inspiring and witty, but instead she said exactly what was on her mind. "Probably because I could be your daughter."

Betsey's face sobered.

"I mean," said Vera, "look at our hair. Both red."

"Right," said Betsey, masking her discomfort with the topic by donning a weak smile. Vera knew at that moment this woman had to be her mother. She had obviously hit a sore subject with that joke.

"Mother," said Owen to Betsey, "this is the woman I've been seeing. Denise." Owen put his arm around Vera.

Mother! That meant that Vera would be on a date with her possible *brother*! Vera slyly wiggled herself out of Owen's shoulder hold.

"Oh," said Betsey. "How did you two meet again?"

"Vegas. And let's just leave it at that." Owen elbowed his mother in a "wink, wink" gesture.

Betsey pulled Owen off to the side and audibly whispered, "Is she an escort? Did you bring an escort to your brother's wedding?"

"Blackjack," said Vera. "I was a blackjack dealer."

Owen looked askance at Vera, his jaw unhinged in disapproval. "Is that what they're calling what you do now?" said Owen. "Blackjack?"

Boy, he really is an asshole, thought Vera.

"So who's this?" said Betsey, pointing at Cole, who was standing off to the side, checking his phone, hoping to go unnoticed.

"This is Denise's brother, Kevin," said Owen. "He's doing some business out here while the wedding's going on, so they came out here together."

"How nice," said Betsey with a tone of indifference. "Well, Denise, you and Owen should get settled at your hotel. Look forward to having you with us this week."

Maintaining composure, Betsey went back into the mansion, presumably to finalize wedding arrangements.

As soon as she was no longer visible, Owen laid into Vera.

"Don't you ever cross me again," he said. "That blackjack story? You're mine this week, and don't you forget it. Into the limo."

Vera had no idea what to say. Technically, she was working for him, so she willfully obeyed, meeting Cole's eyes as she got back into the limo.

"Hey, there's no need to talk like that," said Cole.

"Get in," said Owen. "We'll drop you off at your hotel."

In the limo, it wasn't the cozy, fun atmosphere it was on the way to Newport. It was now stiff and intense, as Owen's attitude had killed any sense of relaxation.

"This week has to go according to plan," he said.

"And what would that plan be?" said Cole.

Owen shook his head, putting his hand to his forehead.

"I'm in love with my brother's fiancée, so I'm hoping to break up the wedding."

"By insinuating you're dating a Vegas escort?" asked Vera.

"That was just to piss off my mom. But I'm hoping to make Catherine realize she's making a huge mistake. If she sees me with someone else, she's going to freak. But"—he made eye contact with Vera—"you have to let me lead with the story."

"OK. Got it."

They dropped Cole off at the Cliffside Inn.

"Call me when you get settled," he said to Vera as he got out of the limo.

The next stop was their hotel, a fancy, schmancy one that had to cost $1,000 for just a night's stay.

After Vera and Owen walked through the hotel's turnstile doors, Vera was awestruck by the hotel's beautiful architecture. Sky-high ceilings, gold fixtures, pristine pillars. She had never stayed in anything beyond a Holiday Inn, and she always thought those were pretty nice.

With her head in the clouds, not looking where she was going, she was unaware that there was a woman with crossed arms storming toward her like a thundercloud. When she finally brought her head back down to earth, the angry blonde was in her face, jolting her back into reality.

"Catherine," said Owen, "this is Denise."

Catherine didn't crack a smile at Vera upon being introduced. Vera noted that this woman looked like the personification of "tightly wound," with her blond hair pulled back into a slick ponytail and makeup that offered almost no color to her already-pale face. In fact, the makeup made her look ghostly.

While Vera was making this mental note, Catherine swiftly moved toward Owen and gave him a quick slap in the face before trudging through the turnstile doors to get some much-needed air to cool down.

Catherine's exit left a breeze, with Vera's and Owen's hair blown back against their heads. Owen gave a wink to Vera.

"It's already working," he whispered.

"Why is she even getting married?"

"She's been with him forever. She'd feel guilty if she left him."

Vera thought of how grim that sounded: a life spent with someone out of convenience. And if Catherine even left him for Owen, it's not like she'd never encounter him again. Talk about an awkward family reunion.

Suddenly, Vera realized that this "him" was another sibling to her. Her very own half brother.

They had reached the hotel elevator, and Owen pressed the up arrow button before they both entered the compartment.

"Hold the elevator," said a male voice.

Vera looked up to see a man that looked a little like Owen—dark hair, tall, and with an air of money.

"Charlie," said Owen. They shook hands. It was a cold interaction, one that almost seemed businesslike and formal.

"And who's this?" asked Charlie, referring to Vera.

"Denise, my lady friend."

Vera shook hands with Charlie, and they rode up the elevator. Weird. She was in an elevator with the brothers she never knew she had, and even though the two of them had grown up together, all three of them seemed like strangers to each other.

"You meet Catherine yet?" asked Charlie.

"Yes," said Vera, recalling the slap. "She's just…lovely."

"Right? I'm a lucky man. So what do you do, Denise?"

"I'm a blackjack dealer in Vegas."

"Cool." Charlie was polite enough, but she knew he was judging her faux profession, as his eyes grew sad and calculating. She wondered what he'd say if she said she had been a librarian—or better yet, a Loan Some escort that provided fabricated friendship to the lonely.

"I'm so happy to have you here, Owen. You have no idea how much this means to me."

"Where else would I be? You're my brother."

This is a painful elevator ride, Vera thought. Not only did she feel uncomfortable with the idea of these two men being her brothers, but she also hated thinking that by the end of the week, relationships could be shattered.

They got off on the fourth level.

"I've got to make a few calls, some last-minute things for Catherine. Great to meet you," Charlie said to Vera before heading off in the opposite direction toward his hotel suite.

Vera followed Owen toward their room.

"He's very nice," she said. "Are you sure you want to do this?"

"We're in love," he said while sliding his hotel card in the door. After the red light on the door blinked, Vera followed him in.

"Are you sure?" she asked. "Maybe it's just lust. The idea of the forbidden. You know, in Nabokov's *Lolita*—"

"I don't want to hear it."

Inside, the suite looked more like a luxurious apartment than a hotel room. There was a work desk area with one of those green library lamps and a computer. Plus, the artwork was not tailored for the everyman: it was classic *Playboy* issues framed quite beautifully.

Vera pointed to these and grimaced at Owen.

"My request. Ask, and ye shall receive."

Then Vera stumbled upon an area that took her breath away. A library. For some reason, although she really wasn't all that surprised given the extravagance of the building, this hotel room had one, complete with an inviting fainting couch for lounging and reading. Vera abandoned her drag bag in the foyer and gravitated toward a copy of *A Visit from the Goon Squad* before lying back on the couch and relaxing with the turn of the first page.

"I'm gonna jump in the shower," said Owen. "Make yourself at home. Although I see you already have."

Just as Vera was about to dive into Jennifer Egan's Pulitzer Prize winner, she heard something ring in her bag. Like a phone. Vera had forgotten that Cole said he was going to pack her one before they left.

Tracking the noise to her drag bag, she finally discovered it in the front pocket. After fishing it out, she held the device in her hand like it was something from thousands of years in the future. With no idea how to answer it, she tapped it a few times like a mother might burp a baby. Then she recalled seeing Cole slide his fingers across his phone a lot, so she copied the action and put it to her ear.

"Hello?" she said.

"How long did it take you to figure out how to answer?" It was Cole, obviously.

"Shut up."

"So how's it going?"

"Well, Catherine slapped Owen after one look at me. So that was kind of enjoyable. And this suite is out of this world. It has a library."

"That sounds awful."

There was a knock at the door.

"Hold on."

With the phone at her side, Vera walked to the door of the suite and looked through the peephole. She let out a gulp after she realized who she was going to have to let in.

Chapter 11

With her phone at her side, Vera opened the door to an angry Catherine, who had her hands on her hips.

"Hello. Catherine, is it?" Vera tried to soften her demeanor with some polite hospitality.

"Where is he?"

"Owen? He just jumped in the shower."

With a swipe of her arm, Catherine pushed Vera out of her way and headed toward the bathroom, not even bothering to close the suite door behind her. Amid the sound of running water, Vera could hear yelling and arguing. It was so loud she worried people down the hall could hear it.

Just as she was about to close the suite door, Charlie appeared. He looked slightly out of breath, as if he had chased Catherine down the hall.

"Is Catherine here?" he asked. "I thought I heard her voice."

"No. I don't think so."

Just then, the sound of running water ceased, with Owen yelling a clearly audible "Catherine."

"Oh. Maybe she is here."

In a similar manner to Catherine, Charlie pushed Vera out of the way before venturing to the bathroom. Vera dared not follow, instead shutting the door and leaning her back against it.

"Stop it!" Charlie yelled.

More arguing, more people shouting.

"I won, Owen," said Charlie. "I had hoped you coming here meant you understood that. Catherine's mine."

Vera hadn't realized that Charlie knew about the nature of Catherine and Owen's relationship.

After some more talk, Charlie and Catherine emerged from the bathroom, with Charlie leading her by a pull of her arm. As they came bounding toward the door, Vera got out of their way, and without saying a word, they left. And then the water turned back on. Owen had resumed his shower.

Vera stood there for a moment, drinking in this utterly bizarre encounter, before remembering she had been on the phone with Cole. She put the phone to her ear.

"Hello?" she said.

"Yikes."

"I know."

"And that's coming from someone who's staying in a cat-themed room. Those guys sound like total shitheads."

Even though Vera agreed with him, she got defensive because they were in all likelihood her half brothers.

"They're not s-heads," she said, censoring Cole's profanity by replacing *shit* with *s*. "They were just, you know, brought up differently than you and me. It's different when you have money."

"Do you hear what you're saying?"

"They can't be that bad."

Cole sighed, kind of irritated with Vera playing this antagonistic game after such a long day already.

"I just wanted to check in. I'm gonna go get in line for the bathroom down the hall. I hate inns."

Cole hung up before Owen materialized from the shower, with just a towel wrapped around his waist.

"We're doing dinner at five. I hope you brought something *not* from T.J.Maxx."

≫ ≪

Just a couple of hours later, Owen stood at the door of the suite, checking his watch every so often.

"Almost ready," said Vera from the bathroom, flushing her T.J.Maxx tags down the toilet to destroy the evidence.

"We're gonna be late," he said. "And Mom hates lateness."

Vera liked the way he said "Mom" so informally. She liked to pretend he was saying it as if he knew Betsey was her mother too.

When they arrived at the Taavi Restaurant, one of the finest dining establishments in the city, the family was already waiting, with two big, long tables reserved especially for them.

Vera and Owen took a seat next to Betsey and another man, presumably Betsey's husband.

"Nice of you to show," said Betsey.

"Oh. You know. We can't keep our hands off of each other." Owen grabbed Vera's shoulder while Vera mentally cringed.

A waiter appeared to take their drink orders. "What can I get you, miss?" he said to Vera.

"A Manhattan."

"Can I see your ID?"

Of all the times for this to happen. Usually, Vera would embrace looking like a twenty-year-old, when she was well into her thirties, but right now, pulling out her real identification was the last thing she wanted to do.

Because she and Owen were already late, it seemed like everyone was waiting on Vera to pull out identification to prove she was twenty-one or older. Vera pretended to be looking through her wallet before deciding that blowing her cover wasn't worth a glass of sweet vermouth, whiskey, and bitters.

"You know what?" Vera said. "I left my ID. I'll just take a Shirley Temple."

Just then, another waiter brought a cocktail to Betsey, setting it down in front of Vera like a carrot in front of a rabbit.

"You really don't look twenty," said Betsey as she took a sip of her cocktail. "That's kind of ridiculous."

Vera didn't know whether Betsey was trying to be nice to her or whether it was a backhanded jab. For some reason, it felt like the latter. Thankfully, the attention was taken off of Vera, and everyone resumed their dinner chatter.

"Denise," said Owen, gesturing to the man sitting next to Betsey, "this is my father, Richard Staley."

Richard stood up, prompting Vera to stand, and they shook hands before returning to their chairs. *Richard Staley.* Vera suddenly realized that her mother had kept her maiden name on Facebook—no Staley. Why would she do that?

"So, Denise," said Betsey, "where are you from?"

Vera looked to Owen, since he was directing the story.

"Las Vegas, Mom."

Betsey looked at Owen as if he were interrupting.

"And did you go to school out there?"

"Yes," said Owen. "UNLV."

"Owen, honey," said Betsey, "let Denise talk." Directing her attention back to Vera, Betsey continued her interrogation.

"Are your mother and father from out there?"

"Yes," Vera answered. "My father's a bartender, and my mother's a drug and alcohol counselor. So one makes them drink, and the other makes them stop." Vera had made this up on the spot and was surprised how naturally lying had come to her.

"But wasn't your father in jail for a while?" Owen really wanted to make sure his mother hated Vera.

"Owen," scolded Betsey, "really?" Turning her attention back to Vera, Betsey apologized for Owen's rudeness.

"Where are you from, Betsey?" Vera asked.

"Small town," said Betsey. "I got the hell out of there at a young age. Never looked back." She turned to Richard, grabbed his hand in hers, interlacing their fingers, and squeezed.

"How did you two meet?"

"I was twenty, working at Clyde's Restaurant," Betsey said, looking at him dutifully.

"And my family came in for dinner." Richard finished her thoughts. "We were from out of town."

"He and I just clicked," she said. "We stayed in touch over the next couple of months, and then his family offered me a job with their corporation."

"The rest is history," Richard said.

Vera recalled Clyde's Restaurant, back in her hometown. It had since been turned into a car dealership. Vera wondered whether Richard had any idea that Betsey had had a two-year-old daughter at home. From the way he talked, Richard had no idea of the excess baggage. Or maybe he just liked to pretend it never happened.

Halfway through dinner, after a couple of rounds of drinks and when the lobster was about to be brought out, Charlie, at the end of the table, clanged on his glass for attention, standing up with Catherine at his side.

"We'd like to thank everyone for being here for our wedding this week, and we'd like to make an announcement." Charlie and Catherine looked at each other with a smile.

"We're pregnant!" said Charlie.

And then he and Catherine waited for a response from the dinner table. Instead, all anyone could hear was the sound of scraping silverware from the restaurant's kitchen.

Owen grabbed a drink and downed it all in one gulp. Betsey rolled her eyes and went for her cocktail too. Looking at each person's face, Vera surveyed the discomfort of the table, and on a scale of one to ten, she'd have rated it at about a fifteen. It didn't appear so much that they were disapproving of the couple conceiving a child out of wedlock but more that they just didn't think these two were "there" yet.

"Betsey, you're going to be a grandma," said Catherine. This caused Betsey to choke on her drink and engage in a coughing fit that caused some of the other relatives to go to Betsey and massage her back.

"This is wonderful, kids," said Richard. "Couldn't be happier for you two." Vera could tell he was trying to overcompensate for the awkwardness. He raised his glass and said, "To Charlie and Catherine."

"To Charlie and Catherine," a table of halfhearted souls muttered.

"Five bucks says that kid's mine," Owen whispered to Vera.

"Five bucks?" said Vera. "You're a millionaire."

At the end of the dinner, as Vera and Owen were walking out of the restaurant, with Owen trying to grab Vera's hand and Vera pulling away, Betsey stopped them and said, "Sailing tomorrow. Eleven a.m."

The *Sightsailer* was a six-person boat used mainly for lounging, even if it was designed more like a racing vessel. When Owen and Vera got to the dock the next day, Charlie, Catherine, Betsey, and Richard were waiting for them, looking like something out of a Ralph Lauren catalog in preppy navy blues and khakis with their hair blowing in the wind. Vera felt a little out of place in her vibrant yellow sundress that she wasn't telling Owen was from Marshall's.

"Morning," said Betsey.

Vera noticed Catherine in the corner, touching her belly. Vera had always found it funny that the moment women announce they're pregnant, they always start clutching their belly immediately, even when they don't have one.

Dinner last night had caused some awkwardness. When they got home, Owen went straight to bed, while Vera stayed up late, reading in the library.

"Some champagne," said Richard, spilling some into two glasses for Vera and Owen.

"Thank you," said Vera. She could get used to living in the lap of luxury.

"Let's get the party rolling," Owen said with a clap of his hands.

Soon, they were off, with the wind taking them out to water. The breeze was so loud and strong that Vera could hardly hear anything anyone was saying. Standing by the edge of the boat, Vera just nodded as Betsey and Richard attempted to have a conversation with her, which was like trying to translate a different language. All Vera could make out was "college" and "liberal arts" and "waste of time." Actually, Vera was pretty sure it was a blessing she wasn't really a part of this conversation. Eventually, Richard and Betsey said something along the lines of "cockpit" and ventured that way.

Out of the corner of her eye, Vera spotted Catherine giving her the stink eye from across the boat. The disdain was palpable, even if Catherine had sunglasses on. Owen, too, noticed the green-eyed monster hiding beneath the shades, and in order to attempt to make Catherine jealous, he made a play for Vera again—this time, grabbing her ass.

"What the hell are you doing?" asked Vera.

There was a struggle between them that looked a little like two children having a slap fight. In retaliation, Owen gave her a push, which launched Vera over the rails and into the water.

Chapter 12

As Vera waded in the water, waiting for Owen to throw her a life preserver or stop the boat, she watched as the *Sightsailer* passed her by, with no indication of stress or acknowledgement that there was a woman overboard. Luckily, since they had just gotten started, they weren't very far out to sea, so the shoreline was within swimming reach, probably a hundred yards or so.

As she made her way toward the shore, Vera did a series of swimming maneuvers she had learned in swim class as a child, including the doggy paddle, the breaststroke, and the backstroke. But she really wished she worked out a bit more—or at all—because she was growing exhausted. However, the fear of sea animals and sharks spurred her to move faster.

As she swam, she also couldn't help but think that her half brother, her own flesh and blood, was so evil that he would jeopardize someone's life by watching her flail over the side of the boat and not offer any assistance whatsoever—just because she wouldn't reciprocate his incestuous advances. Of course, he didn't know they were incestuous.

Finally, she got to shore, her yellow dress clinging to her like a second skin. She felt very self-conscious and crossed her arms as beachgoers oohed and aahed at the woman who had washed up on the beach.

"Mommy, is that a homeless mermaid?" asked one little girl.

"Oh, honey," said the mother. "Homeless people don't live in the ocean."

Eventually, Vera made her way to the boathouse, her feet dripping wet spots all over the cement floor. Her shoes were somewhere at the bottom of the ocean. The young woman at the front desk, with the nametag "Chelsea," did a double take when she saw Vera standing in front of her.

"Holy smoke," Chelsea said. "What happened?"

"I fell over the side of the *Sightsailer*," Vera said. "I was wondering if you could take me back out on a boat to find my party. I don't want them to worry."

Soon, Vera and Chelsea were walking toward the boat docks. As they passed an ice cream stand, Vera spotted Cole licking chocolate ice cream and checking his phone. Like Chelsea, he did a double take when he spotted the drenched but familiar woman walking toward him.

"Owen and I had a scuffle," Vera whispered.

"I'm coming with you," he said.

Chelsea, Cole, and Vera eventually found the *Sightsailer* all by its lonesome, just chilling. As they approached the boat, Vera could see the five passengers drinking champagne.

"Denise," said Betsey, "we were so worried. Our cell service is terrible out here, and we couldn't get a hold of anyone for help."

Yet they all were still drinking champagne, with no indication that they were even trying to find or help her.

"I'm fine," Vera said as Chelsea got the boat close enough for Vera to climb aboard the *Sightsailer*. She turned to Cole. "This is my brother, Kevin. I found him when I washed up on shore."

"Hello," Cole said.

"Kevin," said Richard, "do you golf? We were just talking about hitting a few rounds tomorrow."

"I do, actually."

"You should join us."

Vera loved thinking that while she was presumably drowning in the water, they were talking about golf.

"Owen said you're clumsy and just fell over," said Betsey. "Should we put you in a life preserver?"

Owen wore a sheepish grin as he put his arm around Vera. "Sorry," he whispered. "Don't hate me."

They returned to the shore in the evening, just as the sun was setting on the now-lonely beach. Once they docked, the five family members walked off the boat as coldly as the nocturnal chill in the air.

Vera and Cole let the family walk ahead of them.

"These people are the worst people I've ever met," he said.

"Are they really that bad?"

"You're kidding, right? You were thrown overboard."

"It was kind of an accident."

Cole grimaced at her. "What's with you? You keep making excuses for this family."

Vera wanted to tell him everything, but would that blow this entire assignment? She didn't want to lose this gig and the money.

Vera and Cole approached an empty beach, with the stars popping up in the sky.

"Wanna sit a minute?" she asked.

They sat and watched as the waves kept coming in and creeping back out.

"I have a confession," said Cole.

Vera hated when people said that. It almost never meant anything good. "What?"

"I've never been skinny-dipping." He made a head-nod gesture toward the water.

"So?" Vera kind of knew where this was going but was playing coy.

"So," he continued, "have you?"

"I don't really remember." She was proud she really nailed the nonchalance in this line.

"How can you not remember something like that?"

"Fine. I haven't." She was a terrible liar. She knew she couldn't keep this up too long.

They didn't say anything for a few moments as the sound of the waves easing in and out filled the silence.

"You wanna do it?"

Vera looked at Cole. This attractive, strapping man was asking her whether she wanted to swim in the ocean. Naked. At night. She was typically kind of a prude, but she wasn't a fool.

"Only if you promise not to look at me until I'm in the water." She wasn't a stick figure like Jill, and she didn't want the comparisons.

He rolled his eyes. "It's pretty dark, but fine. You go first." He stood up from sitting on the beach, turned so his back faced the ocean, and waited for Vera. Gingerly standing up and dusting off the wet sand, Vera looked around to make sure no one was on the beach and slipped out of her yellow dress and undergarments before making a run for it toward the ocean. She let out a scream once she hit the cold water, causing Cole to turn around toward the commotion for a split second before reverting to his previous stance.

After a few moments, when the water was up to her chest, she gave him the go-ahead. "Your turn."

"Fine. You can't look either, though."

"Fine." Vera turned around in the water, letting her head tilt up toward the night sky. Within a few moments, she heard a nearby splash and discovered that Cole was in the water next to her.

"Oh, hello," he said.

"Hi," she said.

"This feels pretty good."

"It does."

"Ever get to do this at the library?"

"Sure. I'd walk around naked in the stacks all the time."

He suddenly stopped moving in the water.

"What?" she asked.

"Nothing."

"Are you picturing me naked?"

"Nope."

"Yeah, you were."

"Vera," he said.

"Yes, Cole."

"I don't have to picture you naked. I already caught a glimpse in the moonlight."

She tilted her head in disappointment. "You promised you wouldn't look."

"You screamed. I'm sorry."

"Thanks."

"Relax," he said, scratching his chin with his hand. "You look good."

Back on the beach, Betsey was walking back toward the dock, having forgotten something on the boat. She spotted two figures in the water, and their clothes in the sand. She was especially curious about the recognizable yellow dress, letting out a perturbed scowl.

The next day, while golfing at the Newport Country Club, Betsey kept an eye on Vera and Cole as they joked about each other's swings together off to the side, away from the others.

"Denise," said Betsey, interrupting Vera and Cole's conversation, "you and I are tied for first place."

"Oh, really?" said Vera.

"No one ever beats Mom," said Owen, standing extra-close to Vera, which caused Vera to scratch the back of her neck out of discomfort.

Sitting in the golf cart, Charlie worked on the scorecard.

"Yes, Denise and Mom are tied. Then Dad. Then me. Then Owen."

"Whoa," said Owen, stopping midswing. "Wait a minute. There's no way you're beating me."

"Wanna take a look at the scorecard?" Charlie flipped the card around, and Owen squinted at it.

"Are you kidding me?"

"No. Why would I lie about this?"

"I could think of one big reason."

Suddenly, like a burst of cool air before a summer storm, the atmosphere changed, and it got tense. After standing up from the golf cart, Charlie grabbed a club from his bag. Both men took a stance like they were going to have a sword fight with two six irons. They had both gone overpar with their tolerance of each other.

Seeing her two brothers about to engage in combat, Vera put both arms up in between them and attempted to intervene. "Don't do this," she said.

Then both brothers took a swing.

Chapter 13

$\mathcal{W}$hen Vera awoke, she found herself on a champagne-colored couch next to a shiny mahogany coffee table that had the contents of her entire purse dumped out onto it.

She was all alone in an open lobby area, with giant windows saturated with sunlight, overlooking the green of the golf course. At first she felt slightly embarrassed, having been passed out on a couch in an area where the general public would congregate. But she could tell by the bustle of clinking glasses and silverware in the dish-washing area that the clubhouse dining hall was experiencing a break.

There was a good chance no one had seen her sprawled out on the lobby couch like some sort of bum.

Just then, clad in sunglasses, Cole came in from the outside with an ice pack. "Hey. You're awake."

"What happened?" Vera rubbed her head. It felt like two people were taking dueling hammers to one side of her head.

"Those two nitwit brothers took a swing with their golf clubs just as you interfered."

Vera looked around. "Where are they?"

"The caretaker and I carried you off the green, and then they kept golfing after that."

Vera felt that tinge of anger from before, when she was sort of left for dead in the Atlantic Ocean. But this time, that tinge grew into a heap. She couldn't believe they would just keep playing after hitting her in the head. Despite her fury, she tried to tamp it down and underplay it, mostly for Cole's benefit.

"I see," she said.

"I can't wait until this week is over. You're gonna get yourself killed at this rate. I'm sorry this has been such an awful assignment."

"It hasn't been all that bad." Vera was being truthful. Despite a throbbing head and hands that wanted to throttle her brothers, she appreciated getting to know her family—even if now she, too, was ready for this time to be up.

"What's with you? You defend this family, when they've been nothing but jerks."

Vera massaged her face with her hands. "I need to be honest with you. Sit down."

Cole sat next to her on the couch, taking off his sunglasses because he sensed things were about to get serious.

"The reason I've been so forgiving of these people is because Betsey may be my mother—meaning Charlie and Owen are my half brothers."

This didn't quite register with Cole. "Put this ice on your head." He positioned the ice pack over the goose egg above her right temple.

"I'm serious, Cole." She went on to explain the entire story—from being abandoned as a child to the Facebook search. As the words flowed, it felt almost cathartic to Vera, as she had wanted to tell someone—anyone—this information for days now.

Cole didn't say anything for a long time, digesting everything she had just told him.

"You had Facebook?"

Vera narrowed her eyes at him.

"This is just unbelievable." He ran his fingers through his hair. "I mean, what are the chances?"

"I know. It is like fate."

"Well, obviously, you can't tell anyone."

Vera's heart sank a little bit. Even though she had no idea how she would do it, she had always intended to eventually tell Betsey that she might be her daughter, even if it did go against the Loan Some rules.

"I can't?"

"If anything, you've been given a great gift. You've tested out this family without ever having to commit to them. A lot of us wish we could do that."

"That is an awful thing to say."

"It's the truth. Do you really want to be a part of this family?"

The truth was no, actually. Vera had no intention of becoming a part of this family, mainly because she already had a family at home and because this family was truly just awful. Even if she had wanted to make this her second family, there was no way she could fit in. All she really wanted was just for Betsey to know who she was.

Vera never answered Cole's question; she then turned to collect the items on the coffee table. "Why did you dump out my purse?"

"I didn't," he said. "You woke up at one point."

Rummaging through the likes of Altoids and cherry-red lipstick, Vera finally came across her phone, with one missed call on it. Apparently she had made a phone call while she was in and out of consciousness, and this person had called her back. It was her father's number. Vera couldn't believe she had called her father. *Have I talked to him? Why did he call me back and not leave a message?*

"What's the matter?" Cole asked.

"I called my father and have no recollection of what I told him."

Cole let out a sigh and ruffled his hair with his fingers. "You make my job so challenging."

Before Cole could finish his thought and scold Vera for her recklessness, the door opened from outside, and Charlie, Betsey, Owen, and Richard came frolicking in.

"Denise," said Betsey, "looks like you're doing better."

Vera removed the ice pack from her head to reveal the lump Charlie and Owen's club fight had left behind.

"Have a bit of a goose egg, though." Richard tilted his head to the side in the same manner people ask, "How are you?" when they know the answer is bad.

Owen took a look at Vera and then jumped back as if he had seen a ghost. "Will some makeup cover that?" he asked.

"Who won the game?" questioned Vera, putting the ice pack back on her head and attempting to deflect the conversation.

"Mom did," said Charlie. "She always wins."

"I always win." Betsey lips slivered into a smile. "Better get going, though. Rehearsal dinner."

The Staley family headed out toward the limo, but Betsey lingered behind to watch Cole and Vera. After Vera gingerly stood up from the couch with her ice pack at her side, she and Cole held an eye lock of frustration and exhaustion. Cole kissed his fingers and then placed the spot he had kissed on his hand on her head bump as a sign of friendly affection.

Betsey made a mental snapshot.

Back at the hotel, Vera got ready for the rehearsal dinner alone. While looking in the bathroom mirror, she attempted to cover the bump on her head with mineral foundation and concealer. Nothing was working. In fact, it made her look worse.

She heard the door shut. Owen must have returned. Soon, she felt a presence standing in the bathroom doorway. She turned to it and let out a gasp. Owen was staring at her.

"Why are you standing there like that?" she asked.

"Oh, I just had a conversation with my mother." There was a tone of sarcasm in his voice.

Vera waited for him to continue, but he didn't. "And?"

"And she told me that clearly the woman I am with is in love with her brother."

Vera dropped the foundation container in the bathroom sink. "Excuse me?"

"She thinks you and 'Kevin' are in love. Which, if you are, I don't care, but knock it off. I hired you to be all over me this weekend, not anyone else." Owen exited the doorway, heading toward his bedroom so he could get dressed.

"I'm not in love with him," she said, following Owen.

With his back facing her, Owen turned around and gave her a condescending stare.

"I'm not."

"But something's going on. She pointed out that whenever I try to get close to you, you pull away. And she's right. So stop it."

"For one thing," Vera started, "you are always trying to grope me, so could you knock off all of the horseplay?" As soon as "horseplay" came out of her mouth, she felt like a million years old. Her face scrunched in self-disgust.

"You will recall you're mine this week."

"I realize that. But I'm not your prostitute."

They stood facing each other. Owen's arm slowly became erect, reaching for her butt. Vera gave him a look of "oh no you don't," and he started to chase her in a small circle, with the goal of touching her behind.

"Stop it," said Vera. "I'm your sister." She just blurted it out.

Owen stopped, his face severely sobered. "What did you say?"

"I said I'm your sister." She said it quieter this time, almost as if she were ashamed, which after that little almost-rape chase, she kind of was.

"What are you talking about?" His eyes squinted with intrigue.

"Your mother, Betsey. She's my mother too. We have different fathers. I'm your half sister."

Vera felt like her heart was beating through her shirt. She had finally said it. Each thump of her heart felt like a thousand seconds as she waited for any kind of reaction from Owen.

Chapter 14

Owen shoved Vera out of the way as he made his way to the bathroom. After the quick flip open of a toilet seat, he let out guttural, almost-primal noises, discharging yesterday's and today's meals into the commode. Vera cringed.

Eventually, after a flush of the toilet, Owen came out of the bathroom, wiping his face with a hand towel.

"That wasn't quite the reaction I expected," said Vera.

"What did you expect?"

"Well, not *that*."

Owen ran his fingers through his hair. "I've been telling filthy stories about us to people here for this wedding. Stories about my own sister."

"Serves you right."

"How is this even possible? You being my sister?"

Vera explained everything, from her real name to Betsey leaving her all those years ago to the Facebook profile she spied just days prior.

Owen laughed at first.

"What's so funny?"

"You have two dads."

It astounded her, the levels of asshole he could reach. "And you're so repulsive you had to hire a woman to be your date for a week. Scratch that. Your *sister* to be your date for a week."

Owen's face sobered. "So are you going to tell Mom?"

"No. That's the thing. I can't. I'm not even supposed to tell you."

"Then why did you?"

"I don't know. I didn't want you to have 'sexually assaulting your sister' on your conscience."

"I promise not to try to touch you inappropriately ever again."

"I appreciate that."

"And I'm not that good at keeping secrets. But I promise I'll try not to tell."

"That's comforting."

"Although I think you should. Betsey's always wanted a daughter she could ruin." Owen smirked. "You lucked out. You could have been really messed up like the rest of us."

"You're messed up?" Vera tried to be polite, even though she knew the answer to this question.

"Are you kidding? Look at us."

For the first time, Vera saw Owen as a human being rather than some sort of overprivileged, one-dimensional shmuck she'd read as the villain in a smutty romance novel, one of her guilty pleasures. She had never thought of him as omniscient of his own flaws.

"We better get ready," he said. "Mom's waiting on us for dinner, sis."

At the rehearsal dinner, as Charlie and Catherine made speeches and pledged their love to each other, Owen downed one drink after another, until he finally looked like he might keel over. Instead, he went to the restroom.

"I'll be back," he said.

As soon as he left, Betsey cornered Vera.

"I know what you're doing," said Betsey. "You're a deviant. Using my son for his money. I'm watching you."

Just then, Cole approached them. "Hello, Betsey," he said. "Sorry I'm late."

Betsey gave him a cold stare before leaving the conversation and venturing toward her husband, who was at the bar.

"What'd I miss?" Cole asked.

"Nothing," said Vera. "Nothing at all." She didn't want to make him worry that this assignment was not going according to plan, that the family matriarch thought Denise and her brother were a couple, and that she wasn't with the man she was supposed to be a loaner for.

Owen walked out of the restroom and noticed Charlie and Catherine being affectionate with each other at the head table. After seeing this and becoming emotional, Owen stumbled toward the microphone stand, which was nearby. Grabbing a champagne glass, he clanged it with a fork to get everyone's attention, but he clanged too hard and broke the glass.

"Whoops," he said.

Everyone looked at him with stunned, serious looks on their faces.

"I have an announcement to make," he said.

PART III:

"Put yourself in my shoes."

Chapter 15

All of the attention in the room was on Owen.

"I'm the father of Catherine's baby," he drunkenly blurted out.

Although her skin already made her look like a character out of a Bram Stoker novel, after Owen's revelation, the blood visibly drained from Catherine's face, making her even paler. Her Ivory-girl glow paired well with her overall uptightness. She didn't say anything. She just stewed in her anger.

Charlie rushed at Owen, throwing a punch at him, and the two got into a fistfight. The scuffle was hyperbolic and as epic as Tolkien. The brothers threw each other on tables, splitting them in half like the bloody lips they would both end up acquiring. There were attempted eye gouges, chairs used as weapons, and broken glassware. It went on for many minutes before anyone was able to break them up.

"I'm glad I didn't miss this," said Cole.

Charlie was escorted out to cool off, while Owen stuck around to lick his wounds. With a fat lip and a torn collar, he stumbled toward Vera and Cole.

"At least I didn't reveal your secret." Owen made a cheeky gun gesture at Vera.

Cole's eyes grew wide as he turned to his colleague. "What secret?"

"Nothing." Vera averted her eyes from his stare.

"*That* secret? You told him, after I specifically told you not to."

"It was an accident."

"Unbelievable. I know this situation is a little difficult for you, but you've now made it worse."

"Put yourself in my shoes. Could you keep this secret?"

Just then, Betsey walked into the conversation, catching the tail end of what Vera had said.

"What secret?" asked Betsey. "That you're in love with your brother?"

Cole processed what Betsey had said, mouthing her words like they were a riddle. It suddenly dawned on him who Betsey was talking about. Looking down, he put his hand to his chin in puzzlement.

"I'm going to take a walk." He made eye contact with Vera. "I told Uncle Bruce I'd give him an update on things." He turned and left the rehearsal dinner—although at this point, it was more of a domestic disturbance scene than anything else.

The cops had arrived by this point, probably because someone had reported the fight.

"Hi, officer." Owen slurred his words and made an army salute.

Another cop approached Betsey.

"Ma'am, we're here about a disturbance. Could I ask you a few questions?" This cop had arrived just in time, saving Vera from coming up with an answer to Betsey's "What secret?"

"Sure," said Betsey, giving Vera a note of "this conversation isn't finished" with her eyes. The cop pulled her by the arm and led her to a corner.

Vera decided to get some air, although mainly she wanted to see if she could find Cole. She rang his phone a few times. He could be on the other line with Uncle Bruce, telling him to fire her. After three calls that went straight to voicemail, she walked back to the hotel.

⁂

She had blown it. Faced with impossible circumstances, she had breached this operation. James Bond would have never done this. He would have survived and thrived. Now she was going to lose her job.

After getting changed to go to bed, she peeked out the hotel window to see if Owen had gotten home yet. Sure, she could have waited for him there, but she really didn't want to get accosted by her mother again.

Then there was a knock at the door. After venturing to the entrance of the suite, Vera looked in the peephole to see Betsey. There was no escaping her. She *did* always win. Taking a deep breath, Vera opened the door.

Betsey had a different air about her this time—one more relaxed, less tense. She looked like she was searching for words.

"Are you Vera?" she said with tears swelling in her eyes.

The question hit Vera like a bowling ball to the stomach. Fingering her hair behind her ear, she noticed her hand trembling. "Yes," she said.

Betsey shut her eyes, as if some sort of weight had been lifted from her, before opening them again. "Can I come in?"

Vera ushered her in, and they sat on the fainting chair in the library suite.

"How did you figure it out?" said Vera.

"I think I knew the moment I met you," said Betsey, whose makeup was smeared by now. "But...Owen told me after you left."

Vera now knew what it was like to have a brother tattle on her.

"How did you figure out I was your mother?"

"I found you on Facebook of all places. Betsey Burrows."

Betsey nodded her head as she wiped away tears with her wrists. "I actually took out that account with the intention of finding you."

"You did?"

"It's something I've lived with for more than half my life." She turned her body to face Vera so that they were looking directly at each other.

"I didn't always know your father was gay. He broke my heart when he told me. But when I discovered I was pregnant, I knew I had to have you, whether or not I came from a strict Catholic family. Your father was so supportive, every step of the way. But I was the laughing stock of the town. I had had a baby with a man who would never want me. So when I saw an opportunity to start over, I did." She grabbed Vera's hand. "And I don't regret it. As selfish as that may sound."

Vera tried to imagine what she would have done. While she would probably never understand her mother's actions, she would also never understand what it was like to be in that situation, with limited options in a different decade.

"I see your father did a great job. I'm glad I didn't stand in the way of that."

It dawned on Vera that her mother didn't even know the real "her."

"How do you know Dad did a great job? You think I'm Denise the blackjack dealer who may or may not be an escort on the side."

"I've seen the way you've dealt with my son—er, your brother—the past couple of days. And how you've dealt with me."

Vera took relief in knowing Betsey was cognizant of her dismissive reactions over the last couple of days.

"I know we may never have a typical mother-daughter relationship," said Vera. "But if you'd like, I'd love to let you get to know 'Vera' as opposed to 'Denise.'"

"I'd like that," said Betsey.

Just then, there was a knock at the door. Vera got up to answer it, and peeping through the peephole, she discovered it was Cole. She took a deep breath before letting him in.

"Hey," he said.

"Hello."

"I didn't tell Uncle Bruce. This situation has been insane for you. I should have understood that."

"Thank you." She only hoped he would then leave after this confession so he wouldn't see her having a heart-to-heart with her birth mother. That could really cause him to fly off the rails.

Unfortunately, he didn't sense that Vera was trying to keep him at the door. Instead, he walked right in and spotted Betsey.

"Hi." Cole looked at her as if he weren't really all that surprised.

"Hello, Kevin. Er, whatever your real name is."

"It's Cole." He looked at Vera, whose eyes confirmed what he already knew: the secret was out.

"Let me get this straight: according to what Owen told me, your company loans out people for weddings?"

"For all occasions, really."

"And people utilize your services often?"

"Like you wouldn't believe."

Betsey paused, looking down at her hands, before looking up at Cole and Vera. "Could you do DAR dinners?"

Later that night, Owen arrived at the hotel room like a zombie, climbing into bed with no other purpose than to sleep off the alcohol. The next morning, as Vera clutched his arm on the elevator to keep him propped up, he whispered to her, "There's no way Catherine's getting married today." It looked like the drama of this week wasn't quite over yet.

When they got to the church, Owen wasn't doing his job as an usher very well, especially since he could barely stand. Soon, the crowd filled up, with Cole in the back on the groom's side and Betsey and Richard right up front.

"You need to keep him upright," said Charlie, who Vera was still pretty sure didn't know they were related. Betsey had said she wanted to sit down and talk to Charlie and Richard after the wedding.

Once the wedding actually started, with Catherine coming down the aisle, Vera stood behind Owen on the altar, as a make-shift support beam so he could stand up straight. When the minister got to "Speak now or forever hold your peace," Owen cleared his throat as if he were going to speak, but someone else did for him.

"Stop this wedding," said a man walking down the aisle in a crisp black suit. He looked like something out of a magazine ad, his deep-black skin jumping off the page of this white-bread audience.

The wedding guests gasped.

"Catherine is carrying my baby," he said. "This marriage is a sham."

Charlie turned to Catherine, dropping her hands, which he had been holding. "Are you kidding? You've been two—er, three-timing me?"

Catherine rolled her eyes toward the top of her head, in a disgusted but unapologetic manner. "Yes."

"Move me over there," said Owen to Vera, who was still propping him up.

Vera and Owen moved together toward Catherine with their arms linked, almost like human marionettes.

"Hold my arm up so I can point at her," whispered Owen to Vera. "Catherine, I can handle you being with my brother. He kinda looks like me. But how dare you get with this *GQ*-looking mother—"

"Reminder. You *are* in a church," interrupted Vera, who was holding his right "emphasizing" arm.

"I...I...." Catherine looked around at everyone on the altar before moving toward the *GQ* man in the aisle. "I've made my choice, Irving."

"But my startup just went public," said Irving. "I'm slated to make two hundred fifty million."

Catherine turned to the brothers and said, "I've made my choice, Charlie...and Owen." She grabbed Irving's hand, and they ran up the aisle as the wedding guests booed and threw their programs at her. This had finally given them a reason to hate her, rather than just their general disinterest.

Charlie's and Owen's eyes locked after she left.

"Hey, brother," said Charlie.

"Sorry, man," said Owen, who gingerly walked on his own toward Charlie, without the help of Vera.

"I lost her." Charlie ruffled his hair with his fingers.

"*We* lost her." Owen put his hand on his brother's shoulder.

Charlie's face grew sober. "We? I was the one engaged to her."

Soon the brothers once again rumbled. Given the location, on an altar at a wedding, it was one of their most epic bouts yet. Owen, who was weak due to his hangover, simply lay in a ball on the carpet floor while Charlie threw his fists at him. Vera intervened and luckily ended up not getting injured in the process this time.

"Guys," she said, "you two need each other more than ever now. To get through this."

Charlie looked down at Owen, sighed, and then put out his hand to assist Owen in standing up. After Owen took Charlie's hand, they stood next to each other where the bride and groom would have stood. The congregation applauded at their reconciliation, and even the organist started in with the outgoing wedding march music. Charlie and Owen turned toward the crowd and sheepishly waved before walking up the aisle, shaking hands with congregation members as they made their way to the back of the church.

And just as the church buzz was dying down, with some wedding guests leaving and other family members sitting in the pews gossiping about the events that had just taken place, a lone figure stood at the back of the church, searching the room with his eyes.

Chapter 16

Waiting in the back of the church was Vera's father, standing to the side as wedding guests flocked to the exits. His eyes searched the church until he finally spotted Vera and gave a half-hearted smile and hand wave. Vera couldn't believe he was here. She then recalled the missed messages on her cell phone yesterday, when she was in and out of consciousness. Vera stepped down from the altar and ventured toward her father.

"What are you doing here?" she asked after finally managing to work her way through the mass exodus.

"You called me yesterday. You don't remember?" Despite not being invited, up close he didn't look too out of place with the wedding guests, as he had dressed up like he had been on the list, wearing black slacks, a dress shirt, and a blazer. Vera wondered what she had told him on the phone.

"I had been hit in the head with a golf club, so I was a little out of it."

"That explains a lot." He put his hand to the goose egg on her forehead.

"What did I tell you?" she asked.

Vera's father nodded toward the altar, where Betsey was stand-ing with Richard, probably discussing how much money they had wasted on this wedding.

"Everything," he said. "Loan Some. Your mom. Cole. All of it."

Vera found it strange that in her moment of physical weakness, she had achieved emotional strength and clarity.

"So, are you OK?" he asked.

"Yes, believe it or not."

Soon, upon noticing Vera speaking with a man she hadn't seen in thirty-some years, Betsey gingerly walked toward them. Despite this happening behind Vera, she could see in her father's eyes that Betsey was approaching, by the way his pupils grew intense and nervous.

"Adam," said Betsey.

"Bets," he said.

They just stared at each other for a few moments, until Betsey awkwardly put her arms around him. Vera quietly soaked up this moment of seeing her parents together for the first time ever.

"I met Vera," Betsey said. "She's lovely."

"She is. We like her." As much as Vera appreciated having both of her parents in the same room, it was really quite uncomfortable.

"Could we go for a walk?" Betsey asked Adam. "Just you and me."

Adam met Vera's eyes, almost as a sign of seeking permission. Vera nodded.

"Sure," he said. And Betsey and Adam walked toward the back of the church, out into the courtyard surrounding the building. Vera stood watching them until Cole approached.

"That your dad?" he asked.

"Yeah. Apparently I called and invited him here yesterday."

"Nope," he said. "I did."

Vera turned to Cole. "You did?"

"After I walked out last night, I received a call from your dad. He wanted to know more about the business but mostly if you were OK."

"What did you tell him?"

"I said you were in a tricky situation and that you would need his support through this experience."

"He didn't need to come here."

"He didn't, but he may as well be a part of this family reunion too."

"You jeopardized the company's rules for this."

"I did," he said with a sigh. "But I'm thinking we may have to amend some of the rules."

"And why's that?"

"Well, we've never accounted for situations where you might actually be related to the people you're loaning for."

"True."

"Besides," he said with a smile, "as long as you're around, all bets are off."

Vera matched his smile with a grin. It was just the kind of description of her favorite literary heroes and heroines. Only now, she was the protagonist.